STRIPPED

At bullet speed, things had gone from bad to worse for Skye Fargo. One second he was in the arms of delectable dark-haired Lily—the next, a gang of gunmen were beating down the door.

"Get out," Lily whispered, and Fargo needed no urging.

Grabbing his Colt, knife, and his wadded-up clothes and boots, he headed for the window. He climbed out onto the angled, snow-covered rooftop, three stories above the street, too far to jump. He heard gunfire and started to run—until his bare feet hit ice, and went out from under him.

Fargo belly-slid down the roof, his hands clawing for a hold. His bundle went down ahead of him over the side. Then his feet went over into empty air, and as he started to drop, he desperately grabbed the roof gutter.

The Trailsman was dangling three stories above the main street of Martindale, stark naked. His weapons lay thirty feet below him in the snow. And gunmen were fanning out over the roof now, like ravenous wolves scenting the kill.

It was definitely time for the Trailsman to pull something out of the hat—if he only had one. . . .

THE

TRAILSMAN

154

AMBUSH AT
SKULL PASS

by

Jon Sharpe

A SIGNET BOOK

SIGNET
Published by the Penguin Group
Penguin Books USA Inc., 375 Hudson Street,
New York, New York 10014, U.S.A.
Penguin Books Ltd, 27 Wrights Lane,
London W8 5TZ, England
Penguin Books Australia Ltd, Ringwood,
Victoria, Australia
Penguin Books Canada Ltd, 10 Alcorn Avenue,
Toronto, Ontario, Canada M4V 3B2
Penguin Books (N.Z.) Ltd, 182–190 Wairau Road,
Auckland 10, New Zealand

Penguin Books Ltd, Registered Offices:
Harmondsworth, Middlesex, England

First published by Signet, an imprint of Dutton Signet,
a division of Penguin Books USA Inc.

First Printing, October, 1994
10 9 8 7 6 5 4 3 2 1

The first chapter of this book previously appeared in *Saguaro Showdown*,
the one hundred fifty-third volume in this series.

 REGISTERED TRADEMARK—MARCA REGISTRADA

Printed in the United States of America

The Trailsman

Beginnings . . . they bend the tree and they mark the man. Skye Fargo was born when he was eighteen. Terror was his midwife, vengeance his first cry. Killing spawned Skye Fargo, ruthless, cold-blooded murder. Out of the acrid smoke of gunpowder still hanging in the air, he rose, cried out a promise never forgotten.

  The Trailsman they began to call him all across the West: searcher, scout, hunter, the man who could see where others only looked, his skills for hire but not his soul, the man who lived each day to the fullest, yet trailed each tomorrow. Skye Fargo, the Trailsman, and the seeker who could take the wildness of a land and the wanting of a woman and make them his own.

Colorado Territory, 1860,
where the high Rockies are
snow-white and beautiful as one particular woman—
and just as cold and treacherous . . .

1

The bitter wind of late autumn carried the smell of woodsmoke. Skye Fargo awoke and raised his head, sniffing the cold afternoon air warily, his nostrils flaring. Yes, there it was again. The odor of a fire . . . and something cooking. Unmistakable and not far away. He cursed himself for having fallen asleep.

Fargo turned over remaining prone and careful not to rock the birchbark canoe. Between slitted eyes, he slowly scanned the ragged shoreline. While he'd been napping in the sun, his canoe had drifted the length of the long mountain lake and he was now close to shore. The blue spruce crowded right down to the water, while off to one side a stand of quaking aspen rained golden leaves in the slight breeze. He expected to see a canoe drawn on shore, or a campsite, but there was nothing.

Whoever was camped nearby had hidden the site well. Too well, Fargo thought uncomfortably. And whoever it was had built his fire so that it burned almost smoke-free, at least to the eye. But as the canoe drifted nearer shore, the acrid odor of fire was so strong that Fargo knew he was practically right on top of whoever was there.

Who would be up in the high south end of the valley this late in the season, anyway? He was miles away from the gold-mining stakes, which were far to the north of the big valley, near the town of Martindale. But maybe some prospectors had wandered south into the area. He discounted this idea immediately. Miners were usually slovenly, making camps you could spot from the next territory. This was Ute country, he thought. Maybe some straggling Utes hadn't yet retreated into their winter camp in the Never Winter Canyon. Fargo suddenly felt uncomfortable and cursed himself again for falling asleep on the lake. He started to put his hand to his Colt but quickly realized it would be a mistake.

Whoever was there knew the ways of the wilderness and was, at this very moment, looking out at Fargo's drifting canoe from the cover of the dark recesses among the spreading branches of the spruce. One shot and he was done for, Fargo thought. Whoever it was could pick him off like a sitting duck. On the other hand, whoever was camped so invisibly among the spruce might be somebody who just wanted solitude and no trouble. Fargo realized he'd have to take that chance. There was no other choice.

Fargo sat up and stretched his arms above his head, yawning loudly as though just waking up. He pulled his fishing line out of the water and made a great show of disappointment at the empty hook.

He lifted one of the six speckled golden cutthroat trout which lay in the bottom of the canoe and held it up for a look. Then he lifted his paddle and slipped the blade into the surface of the lake, pushing with powerful muscles. In a moment, the canoe was gliding swiftly across the clear water away from the trees, leaving a subtle wake behind him like the point of an arrow.

As he paddled, he felt his shoulder blades twitch. His muscles were tense and he was ready to spring into the water at the slightest sound from behind him. But nothing moved and the gunshot never came. When he'd gone halfway across the lake, Fargo began to relax.

Since he was in full sight of whoever was camped there, Fargo didn't head directly to his campsite, which was tucked among the rocks at one end of the long lake. No use advertising where he was sleeping. Instead, he beached the canoe on some rocks a distance away. He strung the fish on some line and turned away, plunging into the dark spruce forest.

He'd been riding through the high country of Colorado Territory for a week, making his way slowly down toward Denver City to pick up some more work. He wasn't in any particular hurry, not with a thousand dollars in his pocket from his last trailblazing job. Instead, he'd taken a detour over the rocky defile known as Skull Pass, the only way into the big valley. Here he had lingered, resting, feasting on trout and enjoying the clear chill air and late golden aspen of autumn. He'd planned to stay by the lake one more day before riding out, back over the treacherous pass. He'd already stayed longer than he should have. The first snow of winter would come any day now.

Fargo climbed halfway up a low-limbed pine and hung the string of fish on a high branch, well away from the sharp claws and teeth of any wandering black bears. He descended and watched the golden-headed ground squirrels scrambling up the branches and searching among the fallen logs as he sprinted farther up the slope. They hardly noticed him as he turned and hiked through the dense trees along the ridge. They were intent on their work, fat with the nuts they'd eaten, their fur thicker than usual. It would be a bad winter in the high country, Fargo thought. All the signs were there.

Rather than heading back to his own campsite, Fargo decided to take a look at the unknown visitor. He'd angle around the lake, keeping in the dense trees for cover, then creep in and see what was what. If he was going to remain camped by the lake for the night, he'd rather know who was staying nearby.

A half hour later, Fargo slipped silently through the white papery trunks of the aspen on the hill above the hidden camp, toward the stand of blue spruce. He reached the darkness of their trunks and headed down the slope toward the shore. The sun was setting, the water had cooled, and the breeze had reversed. The wind blew off the lake now, so he was downwind of the camp. He dodged among the trees until he finally stopped behind a large trunk and peered into the somber darkness ahead.

He caught the flicker of fire and, as he watched, movement. An old man in fringed buckskins stood up and rotated a long stick studded with gobbets of sizzling meat over the flames. A spotted mare stood to one side. Fargo was glad for the shift in wind. If he'd been upwind, the horse might have smelled him and given the alarm. Fargo studied the dim figure before him—long hanks of gray hair and a gray beard. A pile of pelts lay to one side of the fire.

Satisfied, Fargo silently withdrew, retracing his steps up the slope. The man was a trapper, an old-timer, traveling alone. He looked harmless enough. And, although curious to talk to him, Fargo knew the etiquette of the trail—never bust in on a man's camp uninvited. Unless you wanted to taste his lead.

The old trapper had secreted his campsite so carefully that it was clear he wasn't interested in visitors. Fargo would respect that, now that his mind was at ease about the man's identity.

Fargo had gone only a short way, and the sun had just set over the mountain, when he heard whoops and gunfire behind him, coming from the direction of the trapper's camp. Fargo halted and listened as the sounds reflected clearly off the water. Several men, with guns. It was an attack.

Fargo wheeled about and sprinted back toward the campsite, drawing his Colt. He plunged down the slope through the dense spruce until he caught sight of the yellow flames flickering ahead. Fargo halted, then dashed from one tree trunk to another, coming closer and closer until he crouched behind a rotting log within twenty feet of the campfire. He rested the Colt on the log and sighted down the barrel.

Two men held the old trapper by the arms, but it was impossible in the gloom to see their faces. The third, a huge blond, poked at the pile of pelts.

"Nice haul," the blond one said. "Beaver. Elk. Bear, even."

"Just take it if you want," the old man said. "And there's some greenbacks and gold in that buckskin bag over there." The big blond looked over toward where the old man was pointing and grinned. "Take it. Take it all, but leave me in peace. I ain't done nothing to you. Hell, I don't even know who you are."

"How much you think we can get for these?" the blond said, still bending over the pile of skins.

"Shut up, Jake," another answered. "Just get on with it."

Jake spun about and fumbled at his belt, grabbed something and raised his arm high. Fargo peered in the dim firelight to see what the man was holding. It was a tomahawk.

"Now, where do you suppose those bloodthirsty Utes would bury this?" Jake asked in a nasty voice, circling the trapper. The old man struggled in the grasp of the other two. "In the forehead between the eyes? Or maybe in the back of the skull?"

Fargo didn't wait for Jake's next words. He

pulled the trigger and Jake pitched sideways with a yelp, grabbing his thigh. The other two men threw the trapper to the ground and took a step backward, bringing up their guns and firing in his direction. They were damn fast. Two bullets thudded into the log, just below where he'd been, but Fargo had already rolled along the ground several yards, keeping behind the log. He came up again, gun blazing, and caught one of the men dead center before ducking back behind a tree trunk. Fargo melted into the shadows beneath the trees and sprinted in a short arc around the campsite to come from behind them. Their confused shouts and shooting covered the occasional snapping of the twigs he stepped on.

He eased himself around a thick tree trunk and looked out. Jake lay swearing by the fire, his leg bleeding and his gun trained on the trapper, who was sprawled on the ground. The other man was firing wildly in the direction Fargo had been.

"Go after him, you idiot!" Jake shouted, his voice an agonized shriek.

The man started forward just as Fargo stepped closer. His boot came down on a dry twig that snapped like a rifle shot. At the sound, the man whirled about and fired wildly toward Fargo. Three bullets whizzed by him. Fargo crouched, advancing and dodging. His Colt spit fire again and again. But the man was dodging too. Just then there was a flurry of movement in the firelight as the old trapper sprang up and vaulted toward Jake. The other man ducked away. Fargo dashed forward into the small clearing. The trapper and Jake struggled by the fire; the other man was nowhere to be seen.

Fargo cursed and kicked out, catching Jake's big gun hand as he brought it around behind the old trapper. Jake's pistol flew up and the trapper pinned Jake's arms, sitting astride him. Jake's leg was bleeding bad, blood darkening his jeans and the ground under him.

"I'll go after the other one," Fargo barked at the trapper.

Fargo slipped into the trees, listening intently. He had gone only a few yards when he heard the whinny of a horse and the scramble of hooves high up the slope. He realized the three men had come on horseback, riding along the high ridge above the lake. And the last man had just gotten away.

With a curse, Fargo returned to the campsite. Who the hell were these men, anyway? he wondered.

The old trapper was still holding Jake down, but as Fargo came up, he saw that the blond man didn't have long to live. The old man, seeing Fargo, got up and stood looking down at Jake.

"Oh, God, I'm going to die," Jake muttered, his face pasty and drawn. The blood was pumping hard out of his leg. Fargo had unwound the kerchief from his neck to make a tourniquet before he realized it was pointless. Jake had also been shot bad in the chest, probably in the tussle with the old man.

"Who sent you here?" Fargo said.

Jake's clouded eyes focused slowly on Fargo.

"Goddamn redskins," he said, anger in his voice. "Living off the white folks. We'll show 'em." His tone of voice changed as he started to go out of his head. "Oh, Mama. I'm going to die, Mama."

"Who sent you here?" Fargo snapped again.

But Jake was beyond comprehension. He muttered incoherently for another few moments, then his head fell to one side and he gazed, blank-eyed, into the fire.

"The other one got away," Fargo said. "Their horses were up the hill."

"Thank you, stranger," the old trapper said. "My name's McCain. I'm obliged to you. I spotted you out on the lake earlier."

Fargo nodded and stood over Jake, looking down. The old trapper spoke his thoughts. "I'd hoped he might live a while," McCain said.

"You recognize any of them?"

McCain shook his head. "Never seen 'em before. But I'd sure as hell recognize that mustachioed one again, that one that got away," he said, spitting into the fire.

Fargo nodded. He hadn't had a good look at the man's face, but he wished he had. And he didn't like the fact that the three men had found the old trapper's campsite, since it had been so well hidden. The three had been dangerous. He hoped there weren't any more of them around.

"There's something real bad about all this," McCain said. Then he was silent, as if he'd said too much.

"They weren't after your pelts," Fargo said. "Or

17

your money. They just wanted to kill you, and make it look like the Utes got to you."

McCain nodded silently, his eyes thoughtful.

"Let's move your camp away from here," Fargo said. "Just in case that mustache comes back with some pals. I'm camped over by the rocks to the north. I could use some company."

McCain set to packing up the camp. In a matter of moments, he had smothered the fire and loaded the pelts onto the dappled mare's back. Meanwhile, Fargo knelt and rifled through Jake's pockets. He found a knife, a few gold dollars, and a tintype, which he held up to the light.

Even in the half-light, the woman's face was beautiful, her dark brows arched high and her full lips parted slightly in a teasing smile. But what really drew his attention was the rest of her. She was dressed in a skimpy merry widow that showed off her tiny waistline. The lacy garment was cut low and clung to her deep cleavage, barely hiding her nipples. She stood in front of a painted palm tree, with one foot on a carved chair and a shawl over her upraised thigh. The shawl was artfully draped to hide her charms . . . but barely. Her legs, slender and shapely, weren't bad either. Whoever she was, she wasn't shy about showing what she had.

Fargo turned the card over and found an inscription on the back: "To Jake, from Lily. Hurry back."

Fargo memorized her face and then replaced the contents of Jake's pockets. He felt something around the man's thick belt. Three more small tomahawks were tucked into his waistband. Fargo removed one and held it up to the light. The jagged mountain symbol and the red lightning across the haft marked it as Ute. Fargo dropped it and stood up. McCain waited by his mare, ready to go. "I haven't even asked your name."

"Fargo. Skye Fargo."

The old trapper looked at him curiously, peering through the gloom.

"I might have guessed that," he said with a smile. "I've heard all about you. You've done a helluva lot for a young fella."

"Let's get a move on," Fargo said. There'd be time to trade stories later, he thought. For the moment, his only thought was to return to his own campsite as quickly as possible. The light had nearly gone from the sky and he suddenly felt worried about his own gear and his pinto, hidden at the far end of the lake. They started off quietly in the gathering dark.

When they came to the far side of the lake, Fargo retrieved the string of cutthroat trout from the tree where he'd left them. He angled down toward the shore, intending to check on the canoe. When he got there, he found it filled with water, a huge hole in the center where somebody had put a boot through the birchbark bottom. A Ute tomahawk was buried in the wooden frame. Fargo saw confused tracks on the shoreline, but he didn't pause to examine them closely. Every moment counted now.

They hurried toward Fargo's camp, but with every step he sensed he was arriving too late. As they neared the tumble of rocks, they left McCain's mare in the trees and approached on foot, scrambling silently over the boulders as the stars came out overhead. With silent gestures, Fargo signaled McCain to stay behind as he ventured forward around the rock cropping and into the concealed vale where he'd camped for the past three days.

It was as Fargo had feared. The gear in his saddlebag had been scattered and picked through. Nothing much was gone. A sharp glance told him that his trusty Sharps rifle still hung almost out of sight among the golden-leaved branches of a nearby aspen. His bedroll had been sliced to pieces and another of the Ute tomahawks was buried in it. The black-and-white pinto was gone. The hoofprints, cut deep in the grassy bank, showed the horse had struggled when the strange men tried to lead it away.

Swiftly, Fargo gathered up his belongings and packed them into the saddlebag. He retrieved his Sharps from the branch and rejoined McCain a moment later.

"They got you too?"

"And they're not interested in stealing," Fargo said. "Just killing and stirring up trouble against the Utes. But who? And why?"

He puzzled for a few minutes over whether Jake and the two men might have hit his camp first and then gone on to wreck the canoe and swarm down on McCain. But he'd been out in the canoe until heading over to spy on the old trapper. And if Jake and his two cohorts had hit Fargo's camp while he'd been napping on the lake, the Ovaro's neighing would have carried across the water and he would have awakened. His faithful pinto never went anywhere with strangers without putting up a helluva fuss. That meant there had to have been two parties of men. The second party hit his camp at the same moment Jake hit the old trapper. The noise of the gunfire had hidden the distant sound of the horse's call.

The thin mountain air had turned cold. Fargo donned a wool shirt and topped it with his buckskin jacket. "I guess I'll track them in the dark," he said.

"Count me in," McCain said.

It was a helluva job, following prints in the rocky soil in the pitch-black, with a cold mountain wind blowing down your neck. Only his burning anger and the thought of the black-and-white pinto in somebody else's hands kept Fargo going, hour after hour.

At times he crawled on his knees on the pine-needle carpet, peering into the darkness until his eyes made use of the dim starlight above. Only once or twice did he resort to lighting a match, since the light blinded him and it took long minutes for his eyes to readjust to the darkness once the match snuffed out. McCain followed in silence, leading the mare.

There had been four of them on horseback. Four against one. Fargo wondered if he'd have managed to survive if they had found him in camp. And also how the hell they'd found his camp anyway, hidden as it was among the rocks. Whoever they were, they were damned good. He'd been lucky they hadn't picked him off when he was napping in the canoe.

Fargo and McCain climbed the slope above where Fargo had beached the canoe, then passed several miles through forested country, emerging to circle the shore of another, smaller lake. Then the tracks wound down a mountainside and along a rock ridge, where the prints finally disappeared. Fargo searched for another hour, retracing his steps in a widening circle, becoming more and more discouraged. They stopped finally at the bottom of the slope of scree on a broad meadow. Fargo walked back and forth in the starlight, looking in vain for the dark smudge of the horses' tracks.

"Let's start again in the morning," McCain said. Fargo knew the old trapper was right. Even if they did find the trail, the four horsemen and his Ovaro were traveling fast. They were miles and miles away by now, and dawn was only a few hours away.

"The Utes' summer camp is close by," McCain said. "Standing Elk's tribe. They'll have already moved to the Never Winter Canyon. We can take shelter there."

McCain led the way, and in fifteen minutes they were approaching a narrow canyon choked with low, dark piñons. As he followed the trapper, Fargo could smell the coming winter in the stiff wind in his face. The first snow would be coming soon, he knew. And the snow fell hard up here in the big valley. If he stayed too long, searching for the Ovaro, he risked being snowed in when Skull Pass was buried and impassable. He shook the thought away.

McCain pushed his way between the small, low trees, moving silently and warily. Then he stopped abruptly. Fargo came up alongside him. McCain inhaled and Fargo did too. There it was again—the smell of woodsmoke in the cold air.

"What the hell are they still doing here?" McCain whispered. "They should have moved on out a few weeks ago."

Fargo inhaled again. "But no cooking odor," he said under his breath. "Fire's out. Burned wood. And the smell of . . ."

He left the words unspoken, but he knew McCain had identified the smell too. The old trapper turned and tethered the mare to a pine. Then they both drew their pistols and edged forward, moving like a pair of shadows in the darkness.

Burned flesh. That smell hung in the cold night air. The acrid smell of burned human flesh and hair. It was unmistakable.

They paused at the edge of the piñons and looked out across the grassy-bottomed canyon. A half-moon, rising over the mountains to the east, spilled light across the meadow, and Fargo saw the dark-ribbed skeletons of burned-out tipis and small wickiups. Smoke from the scorched earth drifted gently in the starlight. They stood looking for a long time, their eyes slowly gathering in the details, the lumps of dead bodies on the ground, the charred

23

circle of grass that extended nearly to the pine trees where they stood. At the far side of the meadow, Fargo saw movement and he tensed, then realized a few horses grazed there. Whoever had attacked the Indian village hadn't even bothered to drive off all the stock.

Nothing else moved. After a long time, Fargo started forward and McCain followed at a distance to cover him.

The Utes had been gruesomely murdered, hacked and burned. Many had been shot in the face. Fargo picked his way across the charred wreckage, noticing that each of the bodies had been skewered with a Ute lance or a tomahawk.

"Same bunch," McCain said grimly, coming up behind him.

"Trying to make it look like Ute killing Ute," Fargo said. "Could it be true?"

"Utes are as sharp as a knife blade," McCain said. "And just as dangerous. But straight as a honed edge. No Ute would turn against another. Especially not Sitting Elk. He is . . . was . . . a powerful chief. I wonder if he's still alive."

Suddenly, Fargo's keen ears picked up a slight rustle. He gripped his Colt and shot a look at McCain. The old trapper nodded. He'd heard it too. It came from the direction of a burned-out wickiup, which was now nothing more than a charred pile of sticks leaning on each other—but with enough room inside to hide somebody. Somebody still alive.

"Come on out," Fargo said as McCain moved off

to the side to cover him. He spoke the words again in the Ute dialect, which resembled the language of the Shoshones and Paiutes.

There was a sharp sound inside the wickiup, and then all was still again. Fargo repeated his words, adding that he was a friend and had come to help. He walked a few step nearer. Suddenly, a figure leaped out at him. Fargo saw the flash of a blade in the dim light and he grabbed at the arm, twisting it easily.

"Let go. Drop it." He grabbed the figure around the waist and felt the softness of breasts and hips. "You're safe."

The knife dropped to the ground and the woman collapsed beside it. Fargo picked up the blade and handed it to McCain, who walked up next to him and stood looking down at the sobbing woman crouched on the ground. She had been brave to attack like that, and Fargo could tell from the tenseness of her body that she had not given up yet. She would wait until they relaxed their guard and then try something else.

"Where is Sitting Elk?" McCain asked in Ute dialect.

At McCain's words, the woman looked up. The starlight fell across a delicately featured face and round black eyes framed by long, tangled dark hair.

"Beaver man!" she cried, relief in her words and face. She wiped her face with the back of her hand and struggled to her feet.

"Waiting Cloud!" McCain exclaimed, belatedly recognizing her. He offered her a hand and helped her to her feet, then stood with his arm around her. She sagged against him, giving up her fear of them. "You are lucky to be alive. Who did this?" The old trapper turned to Fargo and explained, "This is Chief Sitting Elk's daughter."

At his words, the woman stiffened and fear crossed her face again. She swallowed and tilted her head upward as if to regain control of herself.

"What happened?" Fargo asked.

"Most of my people had already gone to the Never Winter Canyon. But I waited here for my father. He rode away three days ago," she said. "To talk white talk with men from the powerful White Chief. And to bring back food the great White Chief promised. He was not here when the . . . when the fire death came. White men with Indian weapons brought the death."

"So Sitting Elk's alive," McCain said.

"There's time to talk later," Fargo said. Just because the chief was not at camp when the attack came didn't mean he was still alive. The sharp smell of death hung like a cold curtain in the chill night air. "Right now, I think we should get out of here. Go find a safe place to camp."

"No place is safe," Waiting Cloud said mournfully. "No place."

"You will be safe with us," Fargo said. "Wait here and I will find horses."

He set off across the meadow and soon returned with a string of four strong horses—one each for him and the woman and two extra for McCain's pelts and supplies. Among the tangled remains of

26

one tipi that had not been burned he found horse gear—Ute leather bridles and several of the high-seated, elaborate Spanish-style saddles the Utes used. Fargo chose the smallest of them.

When he reached the two of them, Waiting Cloud was kneeling in the ashes, moaning and swaying in the moonlight in some kind of ritual prayer. Fargo and McCain withdrew to the edge of the pine trees, redistributed the saddlebags and pelts onto the Indian horses, then waited. After a time, Waiting Cloud arose and joined them without a word.

Fargo handed the horses' reins to her. "These horses belong to you," he said.

"Four horses?" Waiting Cloud said, looking him over. "But I am the daughter of a chief. Have you anything else?"

Her words weren't making sense, Fargo thought. But he decided to humor her. Beside him, McCain shuffled and looked down at the ground.

"The same men who killed your people stole my horse," Fargo explained to her. "But we have some food and guns. Come with us. If you let me ride one of your horses, we will get you to safety."

"Four horses, some food, and a gun." She looked at him a long moment, flicking her hair with one hand over her shoulder. She grasped the mane of the nearest horse and swung herself up. Her buckskin dress hiked up and her long, muscular legs were dark against the horse's pale coat. "I accept your offer," she added. "I will call you Dark of Night."

Waiting Cloud turned the horse's head toward

the piñons, kicked its ribs, and disappeared into the dark pine branches.

"What the hell?" Fargo said.

McCain stifled a chuckle.

"Is she in her right mind?" he asked the old trapper.

"Sure," McCain said. "You came up and gave her four horses. And she accepted your offer. You just bought yourself a wife, Fargo."

"A *what?*"

"Yep. Your wife, Waiting Cloud. Daughter of the big chief. You and Sitting Elk will get along real well. You treat Waiting Cloud right and I'm sure you and the chief will get on just fine." McCain guffawed and clapped him on the shoulder.

"This isn't funny, McCain."

"Sure it is," the old trapper said as he mounted a horse and rode off after her, leading the two packhorses. "Sure it is, Mr. Dark of Night," he called out over his shoulder.

"Goddamn it," Fargo muttered as he watched the old trapper follow Waiting Cloud into the trees. What the hell? His horse had been stolen by a bunch of murderers, and suddenly he found himself married to the daughter of the most powerful chief of the Utes. Fargo knew he was mixed up in something big and ugly—a bunch of men who were tracking and killing indiscriminately, whites or Utes. And snow was on the way; a bad, deep winter that would seal off the valley from the rest of the world was approaching.

It had been a helluva day.

2

Dawn was breaking as Fargo paused at the top of a hill and looked down on Martindale, the only town in the big valley. He'd seen a hundred boomtowns before and they all looked the same. A motley collection of hastily erected board shacks and filthy canvas tents encircled a half-dozen log buildings. A couple of commercial streets sported some buildings with tall false fronts of new yellow lumber. Signs for drinks and food and mining equipment jammed the storefronts and the rooftops. The streets were deeply rutted and thick with mud. On the mountain slopes above the town, gray and golden tailings, broad swaths of broken rocks, marked the mines where men tunneled in search of golden fortunes.

"That's the big city," McCain said, sarcasm in his voice. "Ain't she pretty?"

"First thing we need to do is find the sheriff," Fargo said. He spoke in the Ute dialect for Waiting Cloud's benefit. "He should know about those attacks. Then we need food and rest."

"The sheriff will help us," Waiting Cloud said.

"Sheriff Thomas is a good man. Great friend of my father." She looked down at the town searchingly. "My father has come here to talk about the winter supplies with the great friend. He is here somewhere."

They started down the trail toward town. Coming up the hill was a short, wiry man leading a mule. A pickax stuck out of his saddlebags, and his wide-brimmed hat marked him as a gold digger. He moved aside to let them pass on the road.

"You coming for gold?" the man asked tiredly as Fargo passed him.

"Could be," Fargo answered pleasantly, pausing to look him over.

"Forget it," the prospector muttered. "Take it from me. There ain't no gold in Martindale. Only gold around here is where you can't get at it. Don't waste your time here. This town ain't what it looks like."

The prospector turned and continued up the slope. After a few steps, he turned back around. "And another thing," he said, his voice low and his eyes on Waiting Cloud. "You ain't s'posed to bring no redskins into town. That's the new law. Indians ain't welcome."

Fargo stood staring after the man as he continued up the trail. He puzzled over the remark about the gold, then he caught up with McCain and told him what the man had said about Indians.

"I don't much relish camping in that stinking town anyway," McCain commented. "But we need a tent and some supplies."

30

They continued down the trail until they reached the first buildings. A few early risers were making their way through the mud. Horses and mules were tethered along the street. Fargo's eyes scanned them, searching for the distinctive black-and-white markings of his stolen Ovaro. But it was not there. Whoever had taken his pinto was bound to turn up in Martindale. One store, marked GENERAL GOODS, was just opening for business. Fargo dismounted, tethered his horse, and went inside.

The shopkeeper looked him over and filled his order for a canvas tent, bedrolls, flour, bacon, and dried beans.

"That'll be a hundred and forty dollars," the shopkeeper said, peering over his glasses.

"How much?" Fargo asked in disbelief.

"Hundred forty," the man said impatiently.

"Bullshit," Fargo said. "That's four times what I'd pay anywhere else."

The shopkeeper shrugged. "Then shop somewhere else," he muttered. "And since you're obviously new in town, let me give you some advice." He looked through the front window toward Waiting Cloud and McCain, who sat on their horses waiting for him. "Redskins ain't allowed inside the city limits without special permission. That's the law."

Fargo spun on his heel and exited the store, walking along the shops until he found another one just opening. The prices were the same—outrageously inflated. He bought the tent and bedrolls and decided they'd hunt some game for food.

Boomtown prices were always high because the prospectors, desperate for supplies, would pay anything. And they paid in gold nuggets and dust.

As he exited the store, Fargo spotted the sheriff's office. He walked over and knocked on the door, then pounded on the closed shutters, but nobody answered. He rejoined McCain and Waiting Cloud, noticing the dirty looks some of the passersby were giving her. The law barring Indians inside the city limits was stupid as hell, but there was no use bringing more trouble down on their heads at the moment.

"Let's get out of here," Fargo said.

"I know a good spot to camp, just over that ridge," McCain responded.

McCain led them out of town and along a narrow path that wound along the foot of the hillside, through the winter-yellowed grasses and dark pines. In fifteen minutes, they came to a secluded grove with plenty of grass for the horses and a clear stream.

"I like this place," said Waiting Cloud approvingly as she dismounted. "Thank you for leading us here, my husband Dark of Night."

McCain shot Fargo an amused grin. Fargo realized he'd have to set the woman straight pretty soon. But first things first. They'd been traveling all night, and Fargo felt the heavy weariness settle on him, as well as the gnawing hunger in his belly.

They set to work pitching camp, drawing water, and building a fire. In an hour, they were sitting around the blaze, having eaten the cutthroat trout which Waiting Cloud had roasted with the wild leeks she'd found nearby. She was a damned good cook, Fargo thought as he passed his tin plate for another helping. As she bent over the fire, her lithe body strong under her fringed buckskins, the neckline of her bodice gaped open and Fargo glimpsed the heavy curve of one full breast, dark-tipped.

Weariness tugged again at Fargo. He thought longingly of the tent and his bedroll. A few hours' rest and he and McCain would go into town again. Try to find out what the hell was going on. Waiting Cloud looked up to catch the direction of his gaze.

"My husband is tired," she said with a smile in her eyes. "He must go rest."

Fargo finished the fish and rose, leaving McCain whittling by the fire. He made his way to the tent and rolled himself up into the bedroll. Sleep came quickly.

Fargo awoke a few hours later when Waiting Cloud crept into the tent. He felt her roll herself in a blanket and snuggle up to him. He slowly opened his eyes and saw her face, her large dark eyes watching his face expectantly.

"Look, Waiting Cloud," he began. He might as well get this over with now, he realized. If the woman thought he'd married her, there could be big complications later. Not to mention trouble with her father, Chief Sitting Elk. "There's been some mistake."

Waiting Cloud smiled as if she hadn't heard him at all. With one hand, she reached up and unfastened the deer-horn buttons of her buckskin dress. Fargo sat up.

"Waiting Cloud . . ." Fargo murmured. She continued to look at him, her dark eyes smiling. She slipped the buckskin dress off her shoulders and then downward, exposing her breasts, which were large and swelling, dark-tipped. She reached over and grasped Fargo's hand, lifting it to her bare breast.

"You like?" she whispered. "You like wife?"

Fargo held her soft breast for a moment, feeling himself harden. He reluctantly withdrew his hand. "Beautiful," he said slowly. "But I'm not the marrying kind. No wife. Understand?"

Waiting Cloud's face darkened and the tears started in her eyes. "You do not like," she said unhappily, shaking her head. "I do not understand. I am the daughter of Sitting Elk. Many braves want me for a wife. But I have chosen you, Dark of Night. I saw you are strong man and good man. Now you do not want me?"

"Look," Fargo said patiently, "I don't settle down. After I get these attacks figured out, I'm leaving the big valley. . . ."

Waiting Cloud brightened again. "Now I understand!" she exclaimed. "I will go with you. I can make travois for your tipi. Put packs on the dogs. Waiting Cloud would like to see what is beyond the mountains!"

"No," Fargo said firmly. "No wife." He pulled on his boots and climbed out of the tent. McCain lay

34

dozing by the fire. The old trapper's eyes opened slowly as he approached.

"Have a good honeymoon?" McCain asked.

"What's Sitting Elk going to say when I reject his daughter?" Fargo asked.

"Never can tell about Utes," McCain said, absently patting the stack of beaver pelts beside him.

"That's quite a haul you've got there," Fargo commented.

"I got most of these furs in the next valley," McCain said. "Not much trapping left around here. This valley used to be swarming with deer, elk, moose, beaver. The game's almost gone now, with all the prospectors coming in. A man can hardly find game enough to eat now, much less for furs."

"How does Sitting Elk's tribe get by?" Fargo asked.

"There's a treaty," McCain said, shaking his head. "Sitting Elk's father agreed to let the white men have this northern end of the valley in exchange for regular supplies from the Indian agent. The prospectors don't much like sharing the valley with the Utes, but that treaty protects them. As long as the supplies keep coming, the tribe can get along all right. The Utes stick to the south end, except for once a year around this time when they travel up near the entrance to Skull Pass to get to their camp in the Never Winter Canyon. One of these days, they're going to be squeezed out of the big valley altogether, sure as shooting."

"That's exactly what's happening," Fargo said. "That explains the attack on the village and those men trying to kill us and make it look like Utes did it. If somebody can make it look like the Utes are breaking the treaty, they can run them out once and for all. The question is, who's behind it? And who was Jake? Maybe the sheriff will have some ideas."

Fargo rose and saw Waiting Cloud emerging from the tent. He motioned her over. "We're going into Martindale," he explained. "You stay here. You shoot?" She nodded yes. Fargo handed her his Sharps rifle. "We'll be gone only a couple of hours. Take a blanket and sit up in that rock cropping over there," he instructed her. They couldn't take her to town with them, but Fargo didn't want anybody who happened to wander by to give her any trouble. Waiting Cloud did as he said, and soon Fargo and McCain were riding down the narrow winding trail back to Martindale.

Low gray clouds scudded across the afternoon sky, and a stiff wind blew out of the northwest with a smell of coming snow. Fargo thought about the treacherous Skull Pass, the narrow rocky passage he had traveled when he came into the big valley. In another few weeks, maybe sooner, the narrow pass would be snowed shut for the winter. As Fargo gazed across the bowl of the valley toward the jagged black-forested mountains and the stark snowy peaks rising behind them, he thought of his black-and-white pinto. Where the hell was the Ovaro? Whoever had taken his horse could have already escaped over Skull Pass. Or else they'd try to sell the horse in Martindale. Fargo cursed to himself and dug his heels into the Indian pony beneath him as they came down the trail into the town.

They rode through the jumble of filthy canvas tents and the junkyard of heaped-up refuse that ringed the town. Everywhere he looked, Fargo saw men with pickaxes, their eyes cold with despair or hot with gold fever. Martindale was like a hundred other El Dorados that had sprung up in the goldfields of the West. After the tents came the mud-choked streets between boardwalk-skirted buildings. As their horses splashed through the muddy street, Fargo suddenly spotted a flash of black and white out of the corner of his eye, but when he turned to look, it was only a snowy horse draped in a black saddle blanket.

At the intersection of two streets stood the tallest building in Martindale, the three-story Martindale Hotel and Sporting House, boasting a cupola and a fancy carved cornice all along the top, painted red.

"That looks promising," Fargo said as they rode by. "After we talk to the sheriff, let's try to track down that dove in the photograph that Jake had in his pocket. That one named Lily. I'll bet she's right in there."

McCain nodded agreement. "And Waiting Cloud mentioned that Sitting Elk was making an official visit to the town to get the winter supplies. We'll look around for him and let him know Waiting Cloud is safe. I wonder if he knows yet about the village being burned down? Could cause a lot of trouble." Then McCain pointed down the street. "What's going on over there?"

A long line of mud-spattered men stood outside a yellow-lumber office with a tall false front. The men were milling and jostling for a place. One man tried to butt in and another threw a punch. A fistfight erupted briefly before others dragged the men apart. A sign with fancy colored letters read: GOLD MINES APLENTY. LEASE OR BUY. MARTINDALE LAND CO.

"I wonder if that bastard with the mustache is somewhere in that crowd?" McCain said in a low voice. "While you talk to the sheriff, I'll have a look around. I just might spot him."

They agreed to meet afterward in the hotel bar. The old trapper pulled up his horse and dismounted while Fargo rode on alone toward the sheriff's office. He caught up to a line of five loaded mountain wagons toiling up the muddy street. The wagons were piled with kegs and crates. The lead driver pulled his team to a halt in front of the sheriff's office and climbed down from the wagon. A tall lanky man appeared at the office door. Fargo watched the pair as he angled his horse around the wagons and tethered it near the office.

The tall man inspected the wagons cursorily and spoke briefly to the driver, then signed a paper and directed the wagons around to a side street. As he turned, Fargo saw a flash of gold on the tall man's chest. "You Sheriff Thomas?" he asked.

The tall man turned and look Fargo over, the lines around his bright-blue eyes crinkling. The sheriff's brown hair was just graying at the temples, and his open face was tan and weather-worn. "And who might you be?" he countered.

"Name's Skye Fargo."

"Really?" the sheriff said, his bushy brows raised in surprise. They shook hands. "You're the one they call the Trailsman. I've heard all about you. Now, what brings you here to Martindale? I doubt even the famous Trailsman can break any new trails in and out of this big valley." He chuckled at the thought.

"I'm just passing through," Fargo said. A couple of men brushed by him on the boardwalk and glanced at him curiously. "Can we talk inside?"

"Sure," the sheriff said pleasantly. He led the way into a plain board office with a rolltop desk and a couple of chairs. On the back wall was a thick wooden door with the bolt shot home. Fargo wondered what was behind it. Along the side wall was an empty cell.

"Guess you don't have too much trouble in Martindale," Fargo said, indicating the empty cell.

"Oh, some drunken prospectors sometimes," said Sheriff Thomas as he poured two cups of coffee from a tin kettle on the potbellied stove. "But we don't get too much trouble in this valley." Fargo took the coffee and a seat.

"Well, you got it now," Fargo said. "I was camped over on the southern lake last night . . ."

The sheriff started, his body suddenly stiff and alert. Then the tall man rested back in his seat and took a sip of coffee.

"Southern part of the valley's where the Utes are," the sheriff said. "You had some Indian trouble?"

"Not exactly," Fargo answered. "A couple of bands of men came by and attacked my camp."

"Utes?" the sheriff asked worriedly.

"No," Fargo said. "But they tried to make it look like Utes. A couple of white men jumped an old trapper, and I saw them about to drive a Ute tomahawk into his skull. We killed two of them and another got away. They attacked my camp too."

Sheriff Thomas put down his coffee slowly.

"Shit," he said thoughtfully, his eyes far away. "I don't like the sound of this. Uh, how many of you were there?"

"Just me and the old trapper," Fargo said. "Obviously, somebody's trying to make it look like the Utes are on the attack."

"Yep," Sheriff Thomas said slowly. "This could cause big trouble here in the valley."

"And that's not all," Fargo said. "We followed their trail. They also burned out the Ute village. Killed the last of Sitting Elk's men who were waiting to haul the winter supplies back to their winter camp."

"Burned out the camp?" Sheriff Thomas asked, his voice shaking with shock. "The whole Ute camp?"

"Waiting Cloud said it was white men."

"Waiting Cloud?" Sheriff Thomas's voice rose. "She was there in the village?"

"She hid out and survived. She saw them. But the rest were murdered."

"Goddamn," the sheriff said quietly. He swallowed a few times and then caught Fargo's eye. "She was sure they were white men?" Fargo nodded. "Chief Sitting Elk and I are . . . old friends. We go way back. I guess you could say I've got a soft spot for those redskins. But the rest of the town? Well, let's just say they don't like Indians any more than most men do. That's a real shame." The sheriff smiled. "The chief is going to go crazy when he hears about this. And I'm supposed to meet up with him later. There'll be bloodshed for sure."

"Any idea who's behind it?" Fargo asked.

Sheriff Thomas looked into the distance for a long time before answering. "Yeah," he said at last. "Yeah. I have one idea who might be behind it. I think I can take care of this little problem." Sheriff Thomas put down his coffee cup abruptly and stood. "I want to thank you, Mr. Fargo, for coming by to tell me about this. I'm sure I can handle it from here on. Now, where did you say you were staying? At the hotel, perhaps? In case I need to talk to you again."

"Camped on the old trail just south of town," Fargo said, rising. Sheriff Thomas nodded and started to usher him out the door. "One more thing," Fargo said, turning back. "The name of one of the men who attacked us was Jake. You know any Jakes here in Martindale?"

"Jake? Jake? No. No . . . I don't think so," the

sheriff said. "Must have been somebody from out-side the valley."

"Maybe," Fargo said. "This Jake had a tintype in his pocket. Picture of a woman, barely dressed. Some dove named Lily. I thought maybe the bar at the Martindale Hotel might—"

"Now, hold on there," Sheriff Thomas cut in gruffly. "There is a Lily over there. But I'm sure she wouldn't have anything to do with any killings."

"Sure," Fargo said, wondering what had got the sheriff so riled. "Sure. But she knew Jake. And she might know who his friends are."

"Listen, Fargo," Sheriff Thomas said, his pleas-ant voice suddenly hard and dark as iron. "There's something big going on here. I don't like these killings, but I also don't like the idea of you going around bothering Miss Lily. You go telling this story around town and you're going to cause trouble. You keep this under your hat, see. I've got an idea of what's going on, but I need some time to figure it out. I need to round up some men to help, if nec-essary. Meanwhile, you just leave this to the law. Just forget what happened. You go about your busi-ness and I'll go about mine."

Fargo shrugged and moved toward the door, swallowing his anger. He'd be damned if he was going to forget what happened. Those men up at the lake had been about to kill him and McCain. And those men had his Ovaro. He shook hands with the sheriff and moved off down the street, walking in the opposite direction from the Martin-dale Hotel. When he'd gone half a block, Fargo paused and glanced into a shop window. Reflected in the glass was Sheriff Thomas, still standing on the front stoop of the office, gazing after him.

Fargo continued ambling up the street and then turned off into an alley. He doubled back, striding quickly through the frigid air a few short blocks until he stood before the hulking Martindale Hotel. Through the gathering blue shadows of dusk, the golden-lit windows beckoned warmly. A buzz of voices and the clink of glasses filtered beneath the front door. Fargo entered.

The wide room was hung with red velvet curtains and swags. A gleaming mahogany bar stretched down one wall, and oil flames flickered in dozens of brass sconces on the walls. The smoke-filled air hung heavy and hot, and the tables were crowded. Men in dusty clothes and leather jackets moved among the tables. The din was deafening. A couple of card games were in progress. A bevy of curvaceous women in colorful silks wove through the packed room, and a few were perched on the knees of various men.

"Hello, big man."

Fargo focused on a small brunette who had planted herself in his path. Her décolleté dress of ivory silk set off her coffee-colored skin and dark eyes. He smelled the sharp, sweet fragrance of lemon verbena. She was't Lily though, Fargo thought, remembering the photograph.

"You new in town?" She trailed one finger lightly down his chest and stopped, as if reluctantly, at his belt buckle.

Fargo smiled down at her. "I'm looking for Lily," he said, his voice just loud enough to be heard over the noise.

"Oh," she said with a note of disappointment. "And who shall I say wants to see her?"

"My name's Skye. I'll wait at the bar."

"Oh." The brunette blinked her eyes at him again, then turned away and pushed her way toward the back of the room.

Fargo took a place at the bar and hooked his boot over the rail. "Brandy, straight."

The bartender poured a double shot. "Four dollars," he said.

Fargo started to protest, but then paid ruefully. The price was extortion. More than he'd paid for a drink anywhere, even in pricey San Francisco. The bartender gathered up his money and turned away.

Fargo took up the drink and turned around slowly, scanning the room while he sipped the fiery liquor, savoring it. It would be tough to spot McCain in this crowd. He searched for the trapper's grizzled head, but he was nowhere in sight. Fargo hoped the old man hadn't run into trouble at the land-leasing office. While he waited, the brunette returned and latched onto another man. The doves and their clients came and went, climbing the wide oak staircase at the back of the room.

Between the jostling men, Fargo noticed a carved door below the staircase, guarded by a sullen-looking man with a potbelly. From time to time, men would approach the door and be admitted. Fargo wondered what was inside. Probably

44

gambling, he thought, as he sauntered over. He touched the brim of his hat to the surly, brown-bearded man.

"Got some poker going on in there?" he asked.

"No admittance," the man said. "Private club. Step aside."

Fargo moved to one side as a couple of dapper men smoking cigars stepped up to the door. The bearded man glanced at them and opened the door. Inside, Fargo could see a dim room and a large table lit by gaslight. There was no card game in progress. The door shut again. Fargo felt suspicion rising in him. What were those men doing in there, and why all the secrecy? Could it have anything to do with the attacks? He glanced at the brown-bearded man, sizing him up. The man ignored his gaze.

"Kind of busy tonight," Fargo said. The man grunted assent. Fargo realized he'd have to try another angle. "I'm new around here. Got any idea where I can find some work?"

The burly man looked at him now with interest. "Sure. I got some advice for you, stranger," he said. "If you want to make some real money, get one of these gold claims. Why, just last week a man found a nugget up there on the mountain as big as a fist. Made him a millionaire. There's a strike every day. In another year, everybody in town'll be a millionaire."

"Really?" Fargo said, feigning interest. "You been up there prospecting too?"

45

The man glanced away. "Nah. Nah. I got a job here and I don't got any time."

There sure as hell was something strange going on in this town, Fargo thought. If the gold strikes were that good, no man would be working at a bar. Fargo smelled a lie, and a big one, but he pretended to take the bait. "Well, I sure do appreciate the advice," he said pleasantly. "I'll get myself some land up there first thing tomorrow. By the way, what's your name?"

The bearded man smiled now, broadly. "Joe. But there's a couple of 'em in town, so folks call me Burly Joe."

Before Burley Joe could ask his name, Fargo cut in with another question. "I ran into a man a few days back. I think he was from Martindale, and I wonder if you know him. His name was Jake." Fargo started to describe the man he had killed by the lake.

"Yeah, yeah. I know Jake Keenan. I ain't seen him around for a couple of days, but he's usually hanging around here. I'm sure he'll be in tonight."

Fargo waited another moment and then cocked his head toward the closed door. "So, what's the private club? Can I join?

Burly Joe looked him over once. "The Gold Club," he said in a low voice. "All the big men in town are members. Blake Griffin runs it, you know. He's a real important man in this territory. Got all the connections. But to get into the club, you gotta live here a while. I'm trying to join myself. Mr. Griffin said maybe next year."

They were interrupted when a few men emerged from the club room. One of them took Burly Joe aside and spoke to him, a worried look on his face. Burly Joe glanced toward the door and then nodded. The two of them made their way out of the bar, while another man took Burly Joe's place as guard. In the bustle, Fargo tried to slip inside, but an older man in a gray suit stepped in his path, suspicion on his face, and the door closed again. Fargo shrugged, smiled at the man, and retreated back to the bar, his thoughts whirling. What the hell was going on in that room? What was the Gold Club anyway? If only he could get inside.

"You Skye Fargo?" the bartender asked. Something pricked at Fargo. Something was wrong here. Something bothered him, but he couldn't make out immediately what it was.

"Yeah, I'm Skye Fargo."

"Miss Lily said she'd be along in fifteen minutes."

Fargo drained the last of his brandy and set down the glass. The bartender loaded a tray with a dozen drinks, then moved down the bar to refill some glasses. A harried waiter in a baggy white jacket bustled by. "Goddamn job. Gimme this, gimme that," the waiter muttered.

"Hey you! Get that tray into the club!" the bartender shouted from the other end of the bar.

"Take it yourself," the waiter muttered under his breath. He stripped off his white coat and threw it down, plunging into the crowd. Fargo glanced the length of the gleaming mahogany and saw that the bartender had not noticed that the waiter had just quit. Nobody paid any attention as Fargo ducked behind the bar, doffed his hat and donned the white coat, which hardly closed across his broad, muscular chest. Fargo hoisted the tray of drinks and made his way to the carved wooden door.

The new guard scarcely looked at him and the door opened. Fargo stepped inside and paused, standing in the deep shadow that ringed the room.

A gas lamp hung over the green baize table. About a dozen men sat around, their faces ghostly in the low light. The man at the head of the table was reading a piece of paper. His slicked-down gray hair was parted in the middle and a thick gold watch chain crossed his silver brocade vest. He was small, almost the size of a dwarf, and Fargo realized that his chair had been built up so that he was sitting level with the other men.

"I'm glad to report we're almost there," the small man said. His voice was barely a whisper, and Fargo had to strain to hear the words. So did the other men around the table, all of whom leaned forward attentively. "Another few days and we'll have enough. We'll get it to Washington. The vote will go through in another month. That's a promise."

"When can we expect the final clean-up, Blake?" a man asked. Fargo realized that the small man was Blake Griffin.

"Just as soon as . . ." Griffin stopped suddenly, his dark eyes glittering in the lamplight. "Who is that man?" He was staring into the gloom, straight at Fargo.

"Scuse me. Got yer drinks here," Fargo mumbled. He ducked his head down to hide his face, deposited the tray on the table, and hastily left the room. He could feel Blake Griffin's eyes boring into his back. Fargo plunged into the crowd. By the time he reached the bar, he had removed the white jacket. He wadded it up, stuffed it behind the bar, and retrieved his hat. Just as he sat down at the bar, he felt a hand on his arm. He turned and gazed into the face of Miss Lily.

"Good evening," she said. Her voice was like musical bells and laughter. His first impression was of large dark eyes under arching brows searching his face as if stroking him. Her heart-shaped face, with its small chin and red mouth, broke into smiles. She was tall, very tall for a woman, and her lace-trimmed blue silk dress clung to her tiny waist. The swelling curves of her large breasts spilled over the neckline. A lace handkerchief was tucked into her cleavage.

"Miss Lily?"

"Mr. Fargo."

There is was again, the warning inside him. Something was amiss. Fargo searched his mind for what it could be. "A friend of mine said if I was ever in Martindale, I ought to look you up and say hello," Fargo commented.

Lily smiled and dimples appeared in her cheeks. Her gaze traveled across his face and down to his broad chest, returning again to his eyes. "Why don't we go upstairs, where we can be more comfortable? And you can tell me all about it."

Lily seized his hand and pulled him after her through the crowd. They wended their way up the wide oak staircase, down a papered hallway, and up another flight of stairs to the third floor. She opened a door and he followed her inside.

The bedroom was large and curtained in fringed red velvet. A wide brass bed stood in the center and a carved wooden folding screen stood off to one side.

"Now, let's just get comfortable," Lily said. She reached up and pulled his hat off his head, tossing it onto the bed. "You are a handsome devil," she murmured.

Fargo bent to kiss her, and her mouth opened to welcome his exploring tongue. She tasted of oranges and she purred deep in her throat. He kissed down the length of her neck and trailed his tongue across the swells of her breasts. Her perfume was intoxicating, and he felt himself hard and straining against his Levi's. She glanced down and smiled.

"You got your pistol ready, don't you? Guess you won't need this one." She fumbled at his belt, unbuckling his holster. She stepped away, his gun belt dangling from one hand. "Now, let me just slip into something more comfortable," she said, walking toward the screen. Fargo stood watching as she hung his gun belt on the top of the screen and, with a smile over her shoulder, disappeared behind it.

Something was fishy, Fargo thought. He glanced about and noticed there was no lock on the door. A wooden doorstop was on the floor, and he silently crossed the room, picked it up, and jammed it hard into the crack of the door. Just in case, he thought. If anybody wanted to come through the door, they'd have to break it down.

"So. . . . what's this about a friend recommending me?" Lily asked from behind the screen. She threw the blue silk dress over the top of the screen.

"Yeah," Fargo said slowly. "I ran into this guy named Jake. I think his last name was Keenan. You know him?" As he spoke, Fargo quietly approached the screen. He eased the Colt silently from the holster and made his way back toward the bed.

There was a long silence from behind the screen.

"Jake? Jake Keenan?" Lily's voice was strained. "I don't think I know anybody named Jake." A lacy slip fluttered over the top of the screen. Fargo secreted the pistol under a pillow and stripped off the ankle holster with the Arkansas toothpick, hiding it there as well.

"Really? That's strange," Fargo said. "He showed me a tintype of you. Damned good likeness too. Showed quite a bit of you. Made me want to see the rest." A merry widow was thrown over the top of the screen, followed by one silk stocking and then another.

"Oh, that picture," Lily said with a laugh. "The manager of the bar sometimes passes those out. Sort of advertising, you know?"

"Is that right?" Fargo said. "Well, on the back

you'd written a message. It said, "'To Jake. Hurry back. From Lily.'"

This time the silence was even longer, until Fargo began to wonder if she'd managed to slip out.

"I'm so embarrassed," she said. She stepped out from behind the screen, wearing a transparent black lace robe. Through the fabric, Fargo could see her large uplifted breasts, with their hard pink nipples, and her slender ribcage and waistline. At the top of her long, slender legs was the dark, shadowed triangle. He felt the blood pounding in his organ as he imagined her beneath him. She smiled at the direction of his gaze.

"About this man named Jake," she said, walking toward him slowly. "I'm embarrassed to say I don't remember him. Maybe I wrote that on the back of the tintype, but I really don't remember."

For a moment, Fargo wanted to believe her. He watched as she slowly unbuttoned his shirt. He removed it as she undid his belt buckle and pulled down his Levi's. His erection burst out and she gasped. He stepped out of his Levi's and stood still as she bent over and cupped her breasts, angling his pulsating member into her cleavage. She moved back and forth, his hardness plunging into the warm softness between her breasts.

Fargo held onto the foot of the brass bed as she kneaded her breasts around his cock, then knelt down on the floor and took him into her mouth. Her tongue flicked against the tip, circling it again and again as the waves of pleasure washed over him. Then she took him fully into her mouth, her tongue encircling him with each plunge, her lips forming a tight band around his huge shaft. She purred deep in her throat as he reached down to seize her breasts, pulling gently at the hard nipples.

With one hand, she cupped his balls, tickling him gently, all the while sucking and licking faster and faster on his rock-hard prong. Fargo felt the heat gathering at its base, and he suddenly bent down, pulled her to her feet, and lifted her up. He carried her to the bed and deposited her on it. Lily shrieked with surprise. He stood beside the bed and pulled her toward him, threw aside her black lace robe, and spread her legs open wide. He looked down at her pink, folded, moist portal. Then he grabbed her buttocks and plunged inside her to the hilt.

Lily cried out with pleasure, bucking under him as he put one hand on her hard button and rubbed her, faster and faster, while he stroked in and out again and again, deeper and deeper, her tight wetness opening to him. She writhed on the bed, holding her breasts in her own hands. He pushed harder, feeling himself filling her with his hugeness, feeling her small wet button growing hotter.

"Oh, God! Oh, Skye, oh, oh, yes . . ."

He felt himself about to lose control just as she shuddered and cried out. She contracted and he fell forward onto her, grabbing her full breasts and pumping into her again and again as his own explosion fired into her, shooting deep inside her until he was spent.

After a few minutes, he rolled away. She moaned, turned on one side, and nestled against his chest.

"Skye. That was so good. So good for me," she murmured. "It's been so long since . . . since . . ."

Fargo put his arm around her and stared up at the crystal chandelier hanging from the ceiling. The glittering prisms were like water on the lake. . . .

Fargo awoke with a start. The pounding on the door intensified.

"You in there, Lily?" a man's voice shouted.

"Open up or we're going to bust the door down!" another said.

The first shot shattered the knob, but the wooden doorstop wedged in the doorjamb held it shut. Fargo leaped up, stark naked, and grabbed his Colt and throwing knife from under the pillow. Lily screamed and huddled on the bed. The door shook, the insubstantial wood bowing with the pressure of men battering the other side. It wouldn't hold another minute. Fargo's clothes lay in a heap on the other side of the bed. He hesitated a moment and then dove for them. Lily jumped up and ran to the window. She struggled to open it.

"Get out," she whispered as the door was battered again. "There's a whole bunch of them and they're going to kill you!"

Fargo grabbed the wad of clothes and his boots. There was no time to dress. He climbed out the window onto the angled rooftop, three stories above the street. Too far to jump down. It was snowing, large wet flakes dropping heavily out of the black evening sky. A half inch of wet snow lay on the roof, and it looked damned slippery. Bent low, Fargo sprinted across the raked surface, his bare feet skidding on the frozen snow. He headed toward the protruding cupola and a dark window. If he could get inside and get dressed, he could somehow make an escape down through the crowded bar.

Behind him, through the open window, Fargo heard gunfire and Lily's scream. It would be mere seconds before somebody poked his head out the window and began firing after him. With luck, he could make it to the dark window before he was seen.

Just then, Fargo's bare feet hit a patch of solid ice under the snow. His feet slipped and he lost his balance, fell, and rolled down the roof toward the edge. Holding the bundle of his clothes, knife, boots, and pistol in one hand, he tried to grab hold of anything on the roof to slow himself with the other, but he felt only bare slate and snow. He hit the gutter and felt his legs go off into space. Fargo let go of the bundle, which plummeted downward, and grabbed hold of the side of the metal gutter.

There he hung, three stories above the streets of Martindale, stark naked. His clothes, pistol, and knife lay thirty feet below him. A pack of men were about to fan out across the roof—a pack of armed men trying to kill him.

"He's gone out the window!" Fargo heard from inside Lily's room.

"He went this way!" another voice called, sounding closer. The man was obviously leaning out the window now. "Hey! I see his tracks in the snow here. It looks like he's jumped off the roof!"

"What?"

"Well, let's go downstairs and see where he landed," another voice said from inside the room.

Fargo, swinging from the iron gutter, heard a tearing sound and felt the rotten metal giving way under his weight.

3

Fargo heard the groan of metal and felt the gutter bending and pulling away from the roof as he hung in space. The night air blew freezing blasts on his naked skin. He heard above him the sounds of the men's voices retreating from Lily's room. In moments they would be downstairs, standing in the street below. And then they would shoot him dead.

Fargo cursed and glanced about as the gutter creaked again. There was nothing else to grab hold of, and he realized he could not pull himself up onto the roof without the metal trough giving way. He looked down. Far below him, his clothes and his pistol lay in the fresh snow in an alleyway. If he dropped down, he'd break his neck—or at least both legs. He glanced at the side of the building, wondering if he could climb down, but there was nothing to hold on to. To one side of him was a window, dimly lit. With only moments to spare, Fargo realized it was his only chance.

He screwed his eyes shut to protect them and swung his body once and then twice, felt the gutter give way as he let go of it, then crashed through the window, landing on his bare feet.

He opened his eyes and saw a man with a handlebar mustache between the legs of a redheaded woman on the bed. Both of them gaped at him in awestruck silence. And yeah, Fargo thought, it would be a helluva surprise to have a naked man crash through a second-story window. Before they had a moment to recover, Fargo spotted the man's holster thrown over the end of the bed. In an instant, he had the gun in his hand. The glass had cut his body all over and it hurt like hell, but there was no time to hesitate.

"Move one muscle and I'll kill you both," Fargo warned them. The man and woman stayed frozen in place as Fargo moved quickly toward a pile of men's clothes on the chair. Keeping the gun trained on the pair, he pulled on the man's trousers. They were too short and the waist was too big, but he cinched it with the belt. The boots fit fine though. By the time he was struggling into the shirt, one-handed, the man on the bed was getting restless, his eyes shifting around the room.

"Don't even think about it," Fargo warned, cocking the pistol. The man froze again. Fargo glanced down at his own chest and saw that the glass had sliced his belly pretty bad, but none of the cuts was deep enough to be serious. The shirt was soaking up the blood. Fargo donned the man's leather vest and coat to hide the blood and saw that a wide-brimmed black hat hung on a hook by the door. Over one chair was a pile of silk stockings.

Fargo grabbed them with his free hand and advanced toward the bed.

"I'm gonna tie you up. Sit up," Fargo ordered. The man glanced at the gun and rolled off the woman, then sprang forward, grabbing for the weapon. Fargo was ready for him and stepped aside at the last instant. The man hurtled toward the floor and landed with a thud. He started to struggle to his feet and Fargo coldcocked him. He turned back toward the bed and found himself looking into the short barrel of a silver derringer.

"Now, I just bet you wouldn't shoot a lady," the redhead said. She was sitting up in bed, her pert, pink-tipped breasts exposed above the sheet pulled up around her.

"Not a lady with a gun," Fargo said with a smile. "Or with tits like you've got."

"Nice try, big man," the woman said with a smile. There was a long silence as Fargo and the redhead stared at one another, pistols drawn. Then Fargo heard feet pounding in the hallway and men running up and down, shouting excitedly. By now, the men chasing him had been down to the alley and had spotted the broken window. They were kicking in every door on the hall trying to figure out where he was.

With a fast jerk, Fargo pulled the unconscious man's body onto the bed and pulled up the covers. The redheaded woman waved her derringer warningly.

"If you were going to shoot me, you'd have done it already," Fargo said, as the shouting came nearer.

"You're right," she said, lowering the gun slowly. She smiled. "You're a good-looking man. Got a nice face. I can always tell by the face. Why are they after you?"

"I don't know," Fargo said wearily.

The men were coming closer. He heard them burst into the next room. A woman screamed. There was no more time. Fargo pulled the black hat down low over his face and eased open the door a crack. The hallway was swarming with half-clothed women and angry, shouting men. Fargo stepped out, closed the door behind him, and bumped into the woman in the ivory dress who had greeted him in the bar.

"I've been looking for you," he said with a broad smile. He grabbed her arm and pulled her against him. She giggled and struggled, not very hard, as he backed her against the wall and began kissing her, inhaling her lemon verbena fragrance. The men poured out of the room next door.

Fargo didn't look up as they jostled against him. He moved with the dark-haired woman a few feet down the hall, continuing to kiss her and nuzzle her neck.

"He must be in this room!" one man shouted. Fargo heard them smash open the door.

"God almighty!" the redhead bawled. "First I got some naked ape-man swinging through the window and running off down the hall, and now you burst in here! What the hell's happening to this hotel? It's a good thing my Johnny's a heavy sleeper or he'd shoot the lot of you!"

"Which way did he go?" a man shouted.

"He ran through the room stark naked and went down the hall to the right."

The men poured out into the hallway again. Fargo continued to kiss the dark-haired woman, who ran her hands through his hair. His thoughts were moving fast. He mentally thanked the red-headed woman for covering for him. She hadn't exactly lied, but she'd left out the part about whose clothes he was wearing. That tiny advantage might give him the few extra moments that would mean the difference between life and death.

"He must have gone out back!" The men hurried down the hall. Fargo nuzzled the woman's hair for a moment longer, then breathed a sigh of relief.

"You'd better get out the front," the dark-haired woman whispered into his ear.

"What?"

She smiled up at him and winked.

"When they don't find you out the back way, they'll return. I don't know who you are, stranger, but anybody who kisses like that deserves to live." She pushed him away. "Now get."

Fargo grinned at her and moved swiftly down the hall. He spotted a side stairway and descended. His nose told him it led to the kitchen. He sprinted down the stairs and found himself in a small vestibule where white aprons and hats hung on a row of pegs. Fargo removed the hat and leather coat he was wearing and donned an apron and a tall chef's hat. He pushed through the swinging doors and found himself in a steaming kitchen.

It was hours past dinner, and the only one in the kitchen was an old cook who lay with his head on his arms and a half-empty whiskey bottle in one fist.

Just then the door swung open and four men charged in. Fargo noticed that Burly Joe was among them. Skye turned away from them and reached for a large bowl on a shelf which had some brown eggs in it. He cracked one against the side of the counter. The men glanced around the kitchen.

"You there. Anybody come through here?" One of the other men was speaking while Burly Joe went to the back door and peered out.

"Yeah. Everybody comes through here. Twenty waiters and five cooks," Fargo answered, emptying the contents from both halves of the eggshell into another bowl. "Who're you looking for?"

"Some naked man. Been bothering one of the girls. You see him?"

Fargo bent over the bowl of eggs and began laughing. He didn't feel much like laughing, but when your life depends on faking a laugh, you can sure as hell laugh.

"A naked man—running through the kitchen?" He wiped his eyes and cracked another egg, keeping his head turned away from Burly Joe, who was now looking into the vestibule. "I think I'd notice that," Fargo said.

"Yeah, I guess you would," the man answered. "Let's get out of here, boys. Tommy, stand guard outside that back door. Nobody comes in. Nobody goes out."

One of the men let himself out the back door, and the other three left quickly. When the sound of their footsteps died away, Fargo thought for a moment, then grabbed a crate which held discarded stalks of vegetables and other refuse. He hoisted it and pulled open the back door. The snow swirled in. Fargo spotted the low, dark line of the attached stables off to one side. Fargo walked down the steps. Tommy stood there, his hands in his pockets and scowl on his face.

"I'm supposed to dump this vegetable stuff into the horse's feed," Fargo muttered as he passed Tommy.

He walked to the edge of the building and then turned the corner, out of sight of Tommy. Fargo was continuing alongside the hotel for a few more yards when he heard a familiar voice. He froze and turned away, easing himself along the building until he came to a window that was open a crack. He peered in, careful to stay out of the gaslight filtering through the frosty pane.

"Hell, what kept them?" Lily asked. "They were supposed to come in and get him before I even got undressed. I took as long as I could, and then I figured maybe I got the wrong man. Or maybe they weren't coming."

Lily, now dressed in a dark wool dress, stood beside a marble-topped table. She was talking to someone who was sitting in a large wing chair, which was turned away from the window.

"Look, Blake," she added, "I didn't ask to get mixed up in this. And if Jake hadn't gone off and got himself killed, none of this ever would have happened."

"Now, my dear Lily," a voice said, in so quiet a tone that Fargo could barely hear the words. "I'll make it worth your while. You know I will."

Just then, a knock sounded at the door of the small room where Blake and Lily were. Fargo shrank back as Burly Joe entered. "We found his stuff out in the street," Burly Joe said, depositing the heap on a table. "He's still inside the hotel. We're guarding every entrance and searching room to room. Another five minutes and we'll have him. He can't escape."

"Good, good," the whispery voice said.

"Do you want me to bring him to you when he's caught?" Burly Joe asked. Blake Griffin rose from his chair, all four feet of him.

"There's no need for that," Griffin said smoothly. "Shoot this Skye Fargo on sight. That should take care of our little problem."

"Do you . . . do you have to shoot him?" Lily asked, looking down at the floor.

Griffin glanced at her sharply, patted the front of his brocade vest, and pulled out his pocket watch. "Of course. He's very inconvenient. Now I have some business to take care of, my dear. And then I'll be back. We'll have a late dinner." He reached up and chucked her under the chin as he and Burly Joe left the room and closed the door behind them.

Lily threw herself into the wing chair, and although he couldn't see her, Fargo heard her despairing sobs. He glanced around and saw that the alleyway was still deserted. Fargo put down the crate and began to ease open the casement silently. The window came up easily, and in another instant he was inside.

He took a step toward the pile of clothes on the table and retrieved his Colt. A floorboard creaked under his foot. Lily suddenly stood up from the chair, whirling about to face him. Her mouth gaped open for a moment, and Fargo sprang across the room. He grabbed her shoulders, covered her mouth with one hand, and spoke into her ear.

"I've got some questions for you, Lily." She nodded her head, her eyes large and frightened. "You going to keep quiet?"

Lily nodded. Fargo very slowly removed his hand. She suddenly took a deep breath, and in an instant Fargo brought the butt of the Colt around and gave her a tap on the back of the skull. She slumped to the floor, a whimper all that escaped of the scream she'd been intending. Fargo hoisted her over one shoulder and gathered up his pile of clothing. The alley was still deserted, and in a matter of moments he was sprinting through the falling snow toward the stable, Lily thrown over one shoulder.

The warm, dark interior smelled of manure and leather. Fargo propped Lily against a barrel. She was out cold, and she'd have a bad goose egg on her head when she came to. Served her right, he thought.

Now for a horse. Fargo looked down the long length of stalls and thought of the Ovaro. He pursed his lips and gave a low whistle, hoping against hope to hear the pinto's answering nicker. But, although a few of the horses shuffled, the Ovaro clearly was not in earshot. There was no time to lose.

Fargo saddled up a spirited roan and threw Lily on it. He strapped the knife on his ankle and found his holster belt among the clothing. He strapped it on and bundled the clothing into a saddlebag. Fargo mounted and led the horse out of the stable, staying in the darkness along the side of the low building. The horse was uneasy, pulling at the bridle and balking. It had a helluva lot of spirit. He had nearly gained the street when he heard a voice behind him.

"Hey! Hey! You there! Stop!"

Fargo glanced back and saw Burly Joe sprinting down the alley, gun drawn. He didn't wait, but leaped on the roan behind Lily and gave the horse a swift kick. The roan broke into a run, tearing out of the alley and turning down the main street.

One bullet, then two, whined close by Fargo's ears as he hunched down over Lily and sped down the snow-sodden main street, spattering mud in every direction. The roan pulled hard but had a bad time keeping its footing. Behind him, Fargo heard shouts. He turned around in the saddle just in time to see a crowd of men pouring out the front of the Martindale Hotel and heading for their horses. Then the road turned and Fargo lost sight of them. His thoughts moved fast. His only chance of escape was to make them think he'd headed one direction, and then come around.

The buildings and tents of Martindale passed in a blur as men dashed aside to get out of the way of his galloping horse, then turned to watch him pass. The trail that led out of town forked in the middle of the tents. A hand-lettered sign pointed off to the left and read: SKULL PASS THIS WAY.

Fargo took the left fork. The men following him would assume he was trying to escape the big valley, heading out over the pass. But, Fargo knew, he was in the middle of something too big to leave. Whatever the whisper-voiced dwarf Blake Griffin was up to, it was no good. And Fargo was determined to get to the bottom of it. His thoughts turned to the old trapper, McCain. They had planned to meet in the bar, but McCain hadn't showed. Fargo wondered if the trapper had met with trouble over at the Martindale Land Leasing Company.

The roan galloped on, swiftly climbing the trail among the dark pines leading toward the pass. The snow had turned to hard crystals of ice that blasted in his face. Fargo turned up the collar of the leather coat and fished in the pocket for gloves. Lily was still out cold, and he held her in front of him on the horse.

From the direction of Martindale came the distant pop of guns and the low rumble of pounding hooves. The men chasing him wouldn't be watching carefully, he realized. His pursuers were galloping flat out, and in the darkness, if he turned off the trail, they would not be able to track him except painstakingly on foot. It would be a half hour, maybe longer, before they realized he wasn't ahead of them on the rocky trail leading up to Skull Pass. By that time, he'd be far away. The most important thing now was to find a safe place to hole up for a while. And when Lily came to, to get some answers. Like what the hell was Blake Griffin up to? And why were they trying to kill him?

Fargo turned the roan into the dark forest and slowed to a canter. After a few minutes, he heard behind him the reverberation of the horses galloping up toward Skull Pass. He traveled through the dark trunks of the pine forest until he came to another overgrown trail, which seemed to run on a southward course. He paused and listened to the night sounds. The wind sighed in the tall pines. There was a sudden flurry as an owl swooped down and seized a chipmunk in its talons, then hooted as it flew into the trees. Fargo turned onto the trail, which would lead him around the town of Martindale and back toward the camp where he had left Waiting Cloud that morning.

In a half hour, he tethered the roan to a tree. He lifted Lily down and propped her against a tree, then stripped off his leather coat and wrapped it around her. She moaned but did not come to. Fargo sorted through the bundle of his clothing. He discarded the clothes he'd taken at the hotel and donned his flannel shirt, leather vest, and buckskin jacket. The bleeding had stopped and he could see the cuts were nothing serious. Then, Colt in hand, he moved forward in the shadows beneath the pines until the campsite at the bottom of the grassy hill came into view. It had almost stopped snowing, but the white blanketing the ground reflected the dim starlight.

The camp was ruined. The tent had been pulled up and the bedrolls scattered about. The tracks were visible, but dim. Fargo estimated that the attack had come a few hours before because the snow had begun to obliterate the footprints. There was no one in sight, but he knew that didn't mean there was nobody there. Fargo stood in the covering darkness of the trees for a long time, listening and watching. Then he saw what he'd been looking for—a movement, barely visible . . . the subtle glint of light on the long barrel of a rifle up among the rock outcropping where he'd left Waiting Cloud.

Fargo peered into the darkness, wondering if the Indian woman could possibly be there—or if one of the attacking men had remained behind just in case Fargo doubled back. There was only one way to find out. He angled up through the woods, moving swiftly and silently, until he'd come around behind the rocks. Then he crept forward slowly, easing himself noiselessly among the sandstone boulders, careful not to dislodge any loose stones. As he edged ahead, the bitter wind moaned through the treetops and carried hard particles of ice that blasted his cheeks. Fargo continued on, inch by inch, over the top of the outcropping, until he saw before him the dim figure of a man. For a moment, Fargo considered retreating. Obviously they had captured Waiting Cloud. But something held his attention, and he continued to look at the dark shape of the man before him. The man shifted slightly, craned his neck, and turned his head. Fargo recognized McCain.

"McCain," Fargo said softly. The man jumped and swung around with his rifle. At the same moment, Fargo spoke again. "It's me . . . Fargo."

The old trapper held the rifle stiffly for another moment and then relaxed as Fargo's words sank in. "Goddamn you, Fargo," McCain said, laughing with relief. "Sneaking up on a man like that. I thought I'd keep a lookout for you in case you came back by this way."

"Where's Waiting Cloud?"

"Here," she said with a yawn as she emerged from between two rocks. "We were taking turns sleeping. I am glad to see you, Dark of Night."

"We have a lot to talk about," Fargo said hastily. "But there's a whole gang of men chasing me. We haven't got much time. You got horses?"

"My spotted mare is waiting over that way," McCain said. "I wasn't here when they attacked, but I guess they ran off the other two horses."

"Okay," Fargo said. "I've got a horse up that way. We need a safe place to hide out."

"There's an abandoned miners' shack about five miles south of here," McCain said after a moment's thought.

"Fine," Fargo said. "You lead, McCain. And Waiting Cloud, you ride with him."

"I would rather go with my husband," Waiting Cloud protested.

"There was a woman in town. She's with me," Fargo started to explain. He saw her face fall. "Let's get going," he said brusquely. There was no time for anything right now. They had to find shelter. And he had to get some answers from Lily.

When he returned to the roan, he found Lily shivering and half conscious. He buttoned the leather coat around her and helped her onto the horse, wrapping her in one of the bedrolls he'd retrieved from the ruined camp. She mumbled incoherently.

Fargo followed McCain through the woods as the snow began again in earnest. The clouds lowered until they enveloped the mountains, and the snow drove into their faces and caked on them. He was grateful for the driving, blowing snow, which would obliterate their trail in a matter of minutes. Burly Joe and his gang would never be able to follow.

It took three long, cold hours to go six miles and to find the miners' cabin. During the trek, Fargo's thoughts turned to the events in Martindale. He reviewed every detail of the evening. He thought again about what Blake Griffin had said about sending something to Washington. About Blake and Lily's conversation. Lily had mentioned Jake's name, so she and Blake Griffin were involved with the attacks.

71

McCain led them to the one-room board shack, which had an attached shed for the horses. Fargo lifted Lily down from the roan and carried her inside, depositing her on the bare slats of an iron bedstead. Waiting Cloud lit a gas lamp she found in one corner. She would not catch his eye.

Fargo spent an hour out in the shed, rubbing down the two horses, blanketing them, and filling the manger with the half bag of oats he found behind some discarded mining equipment. By the time he finished, the sky had lightened to pearl-gray as the dawn came, and the snow continued to fall. It was nearly a foot deep already, drifting deeper among the trees. Fargo felt the tiredness settle on him and longed for some food and rest.

The one-room cabin was warm inside. McCain had found some dry wood and made a cheery fire in the potbellied stove. A kettle of water was boiling.

Waiting Cloud sat on one side of the room, shooting dark looks at Lily, who was now conscious and sat on the bedstead, looking about and rubbing the back of her head. McCain blinked sleepily by the fire.

"Good morning," Fargo said.

"Where am I?" Lily asked. "Why did you bring me here?"

"I want some answers," Fargo shot back at her. Then he felt again the weariness settle on him. "But first, we all need a few hours of rest. And some food."

"There's not much to eat," McCain said, fishing

in the large pockets of his buckskin jacket. "I've got a few pieces of jerky and some tea."

Waiting Cloud stirred the tea into the boiling water and the four of them passed the one tin cup between them and chewed on the short strips of dried deer meat that McCain handed out.

"After we rest, we'll talk. And then you and I'll do some hunting," Fargo said, hearing the whisper of snowflakes beating on the windowpanes. Sleep pulled at him and the warmth of the cabin pressed against him like a comforting blanket. Lily lay down on the bedstead. Waiting Cloud slumped against one wall, wrapped in a bedroll. McCain dozed in a chair by the stove. Fargo took one of the blankets and rolled himself up in it, lying against the door, his Colt in hand.

A blast of cold air awoke him and he heard movement. He opened his eyes to see Lily slipping out the window of the cabin. Fargo groaned and McCain sat up, suddenly awake.

"I'll go get her," Fargo snapped.

He rose and went out of the door. It was midday and it was still snowing. The sky was white and the pine boughs bent under the weight of the thick blanket of snow. Fargo strode around the cabin toward the shed and found Lily trying to carry a saddle toward one of the horses. She heard him coming and whirled about, grabbing a rifle and pointing it straight at him.

"Don't you come nearer," she said, her dark eyes wide.

Fargo realized he didn't have his Colt in hand. It was still lying on the floor of the cabin. He cursed himself silently.

"Hand over the gun, Lily," Fargo said, advancing on her.

She raised the barrel menacingly. "I'm warning you, Mr. Fargo. One step more and I'll shoot." She sounded like she meant it. "Hands up."

"Okay," Fargo said with a shrug, raising his hands. "You can go if you want. But where are you going?"

"Back to Martindale," Lily spat, trying to retrieve the saddle while still holding the rifle aimed at him.

"Yeah? Which way is it?" Fargo asked.

Lily paused and then looked frightened.

"And how are you going to get back over Skull Pass alone?"

"What? What do you mean?" Lily asked him, the color draining from her face.

"We crossed the pass last night when you were out," Fargo lied. "Martindale is fifty miles away. You think you can find your way back? And I heard there are Cheyenne Indians around these parts. You want to run into them alone?"

Lily gulped and lowered the rifle. She sagged against the horse and Fargo moved forward, taking the rifle from her. He'd figured she'd never traveled much around the big valley, or she'd know exactly where they were. As long as she thought they were far from Martindale, she'd be less likely to run away. Still, he'd have to watch her closely.

Fargo escorted her back into the cabin, where Waiting Cloud had fixed more tea. McCain rose. "I'm going outside for a time and see what I can see," the old trapper said as he left the cabin.

There was nothing left to eat and hunger gnawed at Fargo's belly. But curiosity gnawed at him even more. He pushed Lily down on the bed. "I want some answers," he said roughly. "Now."

"About what?" Lily asked defiantly. "When they run you down for kidnapping, Blake Griffin will get you hanged," she threatened.

"Right," Fargo shot back. "Let's start with the towering Mr. Blake Griffin. What's going on in his Gold Club?"

Lily stared back, her mouth firmly shut.

"Alright. How about Jake? What do you know about him?"

Lily continued her silence. Waiting Cloud was bustling around near the hot stove. She turned around with a fire poker in her hand, the tip of it red-hot.

"Maybe you need this to make her talk," Waiting Cloud said to Fargo. Fargo glanced at Waiting Cloud. Behind the dark eyes, he could see her cunning. And he could read that Waiting Cloud was incapable of torture. But Lily didn't know that.

"Sure," Fargo said. "Go ahead, Waiting Cloud. I'm getting nowhere with this bitch."

Lily shrieked and shrank back against the wall as Waiting Cloud took a menacing step forward, waving the red-hot poker in front of her.

"Start with her face," Fargo said, adding a laugh he hoped sounded cruel.

"Okay, okay," Lily babbled. "What do you want to know? Please. Please don't."

"Jake. Jake Keenan." Fargo said.

"He . . . he worked for Blake. Was doing some kind of job that took him out of town a lot. Yesterday, I heard he hadn't come back to town and one of Blake's boys said there'd been trouble. That's all I know. Honest."

"Put the poker back on the fire, Waiting Cloud," said Fargo. "It's cooling off and we might need it yet."

Waiting Cloud turned to do his bidding.

"And how about Blake Griffin? What's his game?"

Lily bit her lip and her eyes darkened. "Blake's a dangerous man," she said, glancing around nervously as if she expected Blake would overhear her. "He'd kill me, or worse, if he knew I was talking."

"I'll do worse if you don't talk," Fargo said, motioning to Waiting Cloud who brought the poker back to him. He spit on it and it sizzled.

"Blake came to Martindale just three years ago," Lily said hastily. "The gold mines were all played out. But he said there was more gold up in the hills. He bought all the land for practically nothing and he started leasing it out. Sure enough, there was gold. He was right. And lots of men started getting rich. But really rich. It's because of Blake that Martindale's turned into a real town. Everybody says that."

"Okay," Fargo said slowly. "And what is this Gold Club?"

"That's the group of investors who own the land. A dozen of them put up the money to buy the gold-fields. And any man who wants to rent the land for a while can do that, make his money, and take off. They've got a gold strike every week."

"So I hear," Fargo said.

The whole thing sounded fishy to him. There was the newspaper story about the gold strikes. But if the goldfields were as rich as all that, then no man in his right mind would rent them out. Fargo remembered how Burly Joe had encouraged him to try his hand at prospecting and how Fargo had wondered why, if gold mining was so lucrative, Burly Joe was working in the bar. And there was the discouraged prospector they had met up with who had been leaving the town. Nothing added up.

"And what's this about Washington?" Fargo asked Lily. "I heard Blake Griffin say he was going to send something to Washington."

Lily looked puzzled for a moment, and then her face brightened. "Oh. That's nothing. I guess Blake is sending something to his brother."

"His brother?"

"In the capital. His brother's Mr. Joshua Griffin, the senator from the state of Pennsylvania."

Fargo had heard the name Joshua Griffin. Every-body had. He was one of the most influential and powerful men in the country. Fargo tried to remember what he'd read about the senator. There had been a scandal some years before, some kind of land scam in his home state, but the senator had managed to hold onto his seat in the senate. Somehow, Fargo suspected that with a brother like Blake Griffin, Joshua Griffin was not someone to be trusted.

The door opened and a swirl of snow blew across the floor. McCain entered and stamped the snow off his leather boots. "Saw some deer tracks, Fargo. Shall we get us some venison?"

Fargo reached for his jacket and put it on while McCain warmed himself by the fire. They loaded their rifles, and Fargo took down a length of cord which was hanging on a nail on the wall and took a step toward Lily.

"I'll tie her up so she won't give you any trouble," he said to Waiting Cloud with a wink. Lily protested, but Fargo bound her hands firmly behind her, taking care not to cut off the blood supply. Then he and McCain went outside together. Behind the cabin they found several pairs of webbed snowshoes, which they bound onto their boots with leather thongs.

Then they moved off through the frozen world, walking on top of the soft snow. It took a while for Fargo to adjust to swinging his leg outward with each stride so that the wide snowshoe cleared his opposite shin, but they were soon moving at a fast pace through the pines. Then Fargo's eyes and ears picked up the subtle signs of the woodland animals—the stuttering track of a jackrabbit, the blue flash of a winging jaybird, the distant tap of a hungry woodpecker. They paused at the top of a snowy ridge and looked down into a gentle white valley marked by a gray, half-frozen pond with a thick stand of aspen and bare tangle of scrub oak nearby. At the low end of the pond, Fargo spotted a messy beaver dam and a small, dark form on one shore.

As they moved down the slope toward the pond, the beaver suddenly turned and slapped the water with its tail, making a burst of sharp, cracking noises. Then it turned and slipped into the gray water. On another side of the pond there was a hasty movement as a second beaver plunged into the water at the sound of the danger signal.

"We've been spotted," McCain said with a laugh. "There's deer track all around that lake," he noted. "We can sit ourselves in that grove down there and wait for them to come along. They'll come down that slope from upwind of us."

They were soon comfortably seated on a log in the midst of the shrubs, waiting. While they kept an eye out for any approaching game, Fargo filled McCain in on what had transpired with the sheriff and at the Martindale Hotel, as well as relating what Lily had told him."

"Yeah, I think those gold mines are the key, somehow," McCain said thoughtfully. "I'll tell you, something funny is going on down there. When we split up in Martindale, I first looked over that line of men, searching for that one with the mustache who jumped us at the lake. I didn't see him, but three men came up to me and told me I'd be stupid not to get in on the greatest gold rush in the West. Turned out they all three worked for the land-lease company. It seems the company has a special deal: you rent out a piece of land, and after three months you can decide if you want to rent it again. If you strike pay dirt, the company is obligated to continue renting it to you at the same price. All legal-like. Now, that seems like a pretty good deal to me."

"Sure does," Fargo said. "But what happens if you don't hit anything?"

"At the end of three months, the company takes over your land again. They got contracts and deeds all drawn up."

"I never heard of anybody renting out goldfields," Fargo said doubtfully. "The whole thing sounds crazy."

"Yep," McCain said, his eyes on the snowy hillside before them. "That's exactly what I thought. So I snooped around a little. Some miners had just got fed up, hadn't had any luck, and they were going on about getting cheated. Started a couple of fights and things got out of control. I got off to the side and got in a chin-wag with an old-timer like me, who'd been prospecting all over the West. Asked him if he'd ever run into a man named Jake. He said yeah, he was one of the big guys at the land-lease office. Then I asked him what he thought of the prospecting around Martindale. He was just starting to tell me, and a crowd was gathering around us, when up comes this guy with a brown beard and a big belly, nasty looking."

"Name of Joe? Burly Joe?" Fargo asked.

"Yeah, that rings a bell."

Fargo remembered Burly Joe leaving the bar. He'd probably been summoned to the leasing office to break up the trouble.

"Well, this Burly Joe hears the old-timer talking against the company and he decks him. Put the old man out cold. I got my dander up and I swung a punch, too, and then all hell broke loose. Luckily, in the middle of the brawl, I got away. By this time it was pretty late, so I slipped over to the bar and had a peek inside. I didn't see you anywhere, so I figured you'd come back to camp. I got back just in time to see a bunch of men ride in looking for us. I waited in the woods until they were done. Waiting Cloud stayed hidden in the rocks. Smart girl."

"I wonder who they were?" Fargo said. "Who sent them? The only person who knew where we had camped was Sheriff Thomas."

Fargo sat thinking about the sheriff for a moment. Sure, it was strange that the sheriff hadn't wanted Fargo to find Lily and ask her about the dead man, Jake. But somehow the sheriff seemed like the honest sort. It was hard to believe that the sheriff would send men to destroy their camp.

"I never met Sheriff Thomas," McCain said, as if following Fargo's thoughts. "But I've heard plenty about him from Sitting Elk. The Utes count him as their great friend. They even made him one of their blood brothers a few years ago. That's big stuff for a white man."

Fargo sat deep in thought as they waited in the white cold. Sheriff Thomas couldn't be mixed up in all this. He had seemed genuinely shocked by

Fargo's story about the attacks and had said he had an idea who was behind it. No, Sheriff Thomas was trying to help the Utes and he was on the side of the law. There had to be another explanation.

Just then Fargo caught a slight movement among the trees on the far side of the pond. He raised his hand slowly and pointed and McCain nodded. A dozen bobtail deer moved gracefully across the white landscape, heading down toward the water and the patch of yellow grass on the shore sticking up through the snow, exposed by the blowing wind.

Fargo slowly adjusted his Sharps rifle and looked over the herd. A big buck with a huge rack led a half-dozen does and a few awkward young ones in their first winter. Four young bucks brought up the rear, kept away from the does by the big male.

Two young bucks would provide them with plenty of meat for a while. He and McCain waited, unmoving, as the deer wandered closer and closer. A ptarmigan, white as the snow, suddenly struggled across the snowy expanse, its wings beating uselessly. The herd tensed, ready to spring away, and then they relaxed again, their long necks turning gracefully as they surveyed the silent white valley.

McCain caught Fargo's eye and nodded toward the young bucks. They fired almost simultaneously, the shots echoing through the still air. The two bucks dropped, and the herd of deer bounded off into the woods, a blur of brown against the white snow. A pair of startled mockingbirds flew up into the white sky.

Fargo and McCain stood and stretched their

muscles, cramped from the hour's wait. Then they walked across the snow toward the deer. The two shots had gone true, one into the chest and the other through the neck. The blood ran bright red on the snow.

"Let's cut 'em up here," said McCain. "I'll get us some branches and we can pack a travois for the haul back."

Fargo nodded, and pulled his knife from his ankle. It was bloody work. The warm carcasses steamed in the cold air. They beheaded, skinned, and gutted the animals in short order and were kneeling, side by side, strapping the meat onto the travois, when Fargo noticed McCain stiffen.

He glanced up, following the old trapper's gaze. Coming down the slope straight at them at a fast, off-kilter, loping run was a huge grizzly bear. Fargo glanced about and realized their two rifles were a good fifteen feet away, balanced against a log. In a flash he realized they weren't going to make it.

4

"What the hell?" McCain muttered, jumping to his feet.

The grizzly was running full-out with a sideways, lurching gait, head low and soundless, straight for them. And straight for the bloody carcasses of the butchered deer, thought Fargo in a flash. He scrambled toward the rifles as McCain took off in the other direction.

Fargo realized that by the time he got to their rifles, the bear would have barreled into him. He glanced up for a split second and saw the bear veering toward McCain. Fargo grasped his Sharps just as he heard McCain cry out. He whirled about, raising the barrel of the rifle upward.

McCain had slipped down in the snow and the grizzly loomed over him, jaws wide over the back of McCain's neck. Fargo fired and the bullet, aimed a few inches too low, hurtled into the bear's thick shoulder. The grizzly recoiled and turned its massive shaggy head, deep eyes cold, as if looking for the source of this distraction.

Fargo swiftly reloaded. The bear hesitated and

then charged, barreling at him. He had one shot, he realized, and it would have to be true. He aimed straight between the grizzly's eyes and pulled the trigger.

The shot exploded but it did not slow the oncoming grizzly, which hurtled toward him, all thousand pounds of it, knocking him flat. Fargo felt the deep sting of bear claws raked against his arm as he tumbled into the snow. The bear collapsed, half on Fargo, a huge warm hulk, breathing heavily once, twice, and then not again.

Fargo lay trapped beneath the dead grizzly, pressed into the snow. McCain came running up and knelt beside him.

"You alive, Fargo?" he asked.

"Get this goddamn thing off me," Fargo answered. Between the two of them, they pushed and pulled the heavy carcass away and Fargo slipped out from beneath it. No broken bones. Nothing more than some nasty looking tears in his forearm from the grizzly's sharp claws. McCain was battered, with a nasty scratch down one cheek.

"Now go figure. I thought we were lucky to find a herd of deer in this valley, and now we got us bear meat, too," McCain said, looking down at the grizzly and shaking his head. "The hunting's been notoriously bad in these parts the last few years, but we just had a lot of luck."

Fargo knelt and felt along the side of the bear. Under the thick, silver-tipped brown fur, the grizzly's ribs were prominent.

"Look there," Fargo said, pointing at the bear's

back leg. An old bullet wound, maybe a month old, had only partially healed. "This bear was hungry. It got shot and it's had a hard time finding food with that bad leg. That's why it took the risk and rushed us."

They spent the next two hours skinning and butchering the bear and loading a second travois with the fresh, steaming meat. Fargo cut off the bear's paws to take to Waiting Cloud, since the Utes used the claws for necklaces and various other ornaments.

As the day waned, they headed back to the cabin, dragging the two heavy travois behind them. The milky clouds dropped down onto the mountains and the snow began falling again, the wind blowing hard. When the cabin came into view, Waiting Cloud emerged and ran toward them, delighted.

"Dark of Night and Beaver Man are great hunters!" she exclaimed. She saw to their wounds, bandaging them with strips of sheets, then pulled a knife from her belt and expertly sliced large hunks of bear meat. She also took one of the deer's haunches and ribs. She thanked Fargo for bringing back the bear paws and promised to make him a deerskin shirt decorated with the claws.

Waiting Cloud went back inside. Fargo found some rope in the shed and tied one end to a small rock. He found a pine tree with high branches and threw the rock over one of them. Meanwhile, McCain had tied the meat into bundles. They hoisted it up so it hung more than a dozen feet off the ground, well out of reach of any wandering bears.

It was dark when they entered the cabin. The close room was filled with the delicious smell of meat roasted with herbs, wild onions, and dried rosehips, which Waiting Cloud had found under the snow in the woods.

After two helpings, Fargo sat leaning against the wall, tired and contented, as Waiting Cloud passed him another plate. "You sure can cook," he said gratefully.

Waiting Cloud beamed at him, then frowned when Lily piped up. "Just how long do you plan on keeping me here?" She was sitting on the iron bedstead, wrapped in a blanket, misery on her face.

"Dark of Night will keep you here as long as he wants," Waiting Cloud snapped. "Then he will send you away." She turned back to the stove angrily. Fargo smiled to himself. The Indian woman was none too happy at the intrusion of Lily.

Waiting Cloud had found some horehound bark and made a pot of fragrant tea. After the hot drink and all the meat, Fargo felt completely satisfied and relaxed. As a precaution, he tied one of Lily's wrists to the bedstead with a series of complicated, tight knots. It was possible she could loosen them with her other hand, but at the very least it would slow her down. He and McCain sat by the fire and talked, while Waiting Cloud and Lily, on opposite sides of the small cabin, wrapped themselves in blankets and soon were asleep.

"Damn good luck we had," McCain said with a

belch. He was chewing on a piece of horehound bark. "There used to be a whole lot of grizzlies in this valley, but now they've mostly been hunted down." The old trapper looked meditatively into the fire as if the past were before his eyes. "Ten years ago in this very valley, I witnessed the weirdest grizzly attack I ever saw. It was right south of here." He nodded toward the sleeping form of Waiting Cloud. "And it involved her father, Sitting Elk, before he became chief. I didn't know him in those days. In fact, I hadn't made friends with any of the Utes yet.

"One day, I had just come to the top of a ridge. Down below, I saw this Indian—I later found out it was Sitting Elk—by the lake doing some kind of praying. You know, he had all those feathers and war paint on him. He was looking up to the sky and chanting; every once in a while, he'd stamp around a little like he was in some kind of trance. Well, I thought, better not to interrupt him. So I sat down in the bushes and watched. Now, this went on for a good while. And then off to the side I see this other man, white guy, skinny fellow, creeping up. He's got his gun raised, and goddamn, it looks like he's out hunting redskin. I could see he was about to bag Sitting Elk just for the pleasure of shooting him.

"Well, I raised my rifle real slow, intending to plug that fellow before he murdered that Indian in cold blood. Just then there was a growl, and goddamn it again, if a big old brown bear didn't rise up out of the chokecherry bushes! Well, that skinny fellow, he just wheels around and plugs that bear fast. Then he turns and the Indian's standing there looking at him. He starts to raise his rifle and it was like Utes suddenly sprouted out of the earth. They appeared from all sides and surrounded that skinny fellow, and he was looking all around, stuck as a jackrabbit in a snare. I started getting a little itchy, because I didn't know the Utes then and I didn't like the fact that they were suddenly popping up all over the place. So I backed out of that bush as fast as I could. But I always wondered what they did to that fellow. Every time I see Sitting Elk, I forget to ask him."

"Good story," Fargo said, and told one of his own about the bear that gave him the half-moon scar on his forearm. They traded bear stories into the night, until exhaustion claimed them. Fargo rose finally and pulled off his boots. Despite the fire, the frigid air crept in beneath the door and round the windowpanes, which were thick with frost. McCain stretched out in a blanket near the bedstead.

Fargo lay down in his bedroll by the door and was almost asleep when he heard someone moving across the floor. A dark form came to lie down beside him. It was Waiting Cloud. She did not say a word, but stretched out in her blanket. He could sense that she waited there in the darkness, offering herself. Fargo came fully awake now, thinking of the beautiful woman's strong body, her muscular thighs, the dark-tipped breasts he had glimpsed beneath her buckskins. He reached out a hand slowly, but then thought better of it. Hell, if he made love to Waiting Cloud, there'd be complications—more than there were already. He wasn't sure about the Ute's marriage laws, but her father, the chief, would be none too happy if he took her to bed and then discarded her.

Fargo lay in the darkness, inches from Waiting Cloud. He felt the blood beat hot within him. Sleep was a long time coming.

In the morning, the snow let up for a while. McCain bundled himself in his coat.

"I'm going to keep watch at the head of this valley," said the trapper, "in case those Martindale men get the grand idea to look for us."

When the door closed behind McCain, Waiting Cloud approached. "How is the bear mark this morning?" she asked, concern in her beautiful face.

Fargo held up his arm and she bent over it, removing the bandages slowly. She pushed up his sleeve and caught her breath when she saw the dried blood from the cuts he'd acquired from the shattering window glass back in Martindale. Fargo realized it had been two days and he'd not even washed the wounds, though he could feel from the stiffness of the dried blood beneath his clothing that the cuts had all closed.

"I will make some warm water," Waiting Cloud said. She put a pot of water on to boil and then filled a large tin pot with snow. When the water was ready, Fargo removed his shirt and sat on the wooden chair. Waiting Cloud sponged off his back and chest gently. Lily, lying on the bed, one wrist tied to the bedstead, looked at them darkly.

"Beaver Man told me you are a famous wanderer," Waiting Cloud said as she daubed at his side.

"They call me the Trailsman," Fargo replied, smiling at her.

"And you go alone," Waiting Cloud said. "I have come to understand that. I know that you cannot be my husband because you are a wanderer . . . alone. But does that mean you do not enjoy women?"

Fargo laughed. "No," he said. "I just don't marry them."

Waiting Cloud nodded, her eyes serious. The warm water and Waiting Cloud's tender ministrations relaxed Fargo. He closed his eyes as she worked over him, sponging, drying, and bandaging. As she bent near him, he inhaled the sweet odor of her—herbs and smoke—and felt himself aroused, hardening.

"Take off the rest," she said softly after a while.

Fargo opened his eyes slowly and stood, stripping off his Levi's. Waiting Cloud's eyes widened as she took in the sight of him and she smiled impishly, motioning him to lie down on the bedroll on the floor, face down. The scratches and cuts on his thighs and shins took only a few moments to clean, then she gently sat astride him and began to massage his back and shoulders in smooth, deep motions.

Fargo felt himself melting as he concentrated on

the sensations created by her probing fingers. Then he became aware of the feel of her sitting on his buttocks, her deerskin skirt hiked up and her warm thighs around him. He could feel the slight warmth of her in the center of his back, and after a moment he reached his hand around and felt for her, sliding his hand beneath the bunched up deerskin and finding her wet bush.

Waiting Cloud's hands scarcely paused as she hummed low in her throat and raised herself slightly off him. He gently rotated his finger against her moist lips, then plunged his finger inside her.

"Ah, ah," Waiting Cloud uttered, and lifted herself to her knees. Fargo flipped onto his back, his erect penis standing straight up, hard and ready. He drew her down toward him and she lowered herself onto his huge shaft, taking him fully inside her tight wetness.

To hell with Lily, Fargo thought. She could watch or not, for all he cared. She'd been completely deceitful, setting him up that way back at the hotel. He didn't glance toward the bed, but watched as Waiting Cloud, still sitting on top of him, slowly pushed her buckskin dress off over her head. Her body was golden and warm, her large breasts dark-tipped and firm. She smiled down at him, her eyes shining, as she loosed her long black hair from the leather thong so that it cascaded over her shoulders.

Fargo drew her down toward him and she fell forward, kissing him. Her mouth was honey-sweet and her breasts were warm in his hands. Her firm hips moved slowly, deliciously, as she took him into her, again and again. He felt his hardness filling her and tightening as she stroked him up and down, faster and faster, bucking on him. He thrust upward with his hips and she seemed to open deeper, taking him in. Fargo reached over and put his hand on her folds, stroking, tickling. Waiting Cloud closed her eyes in ecstasy and thrust against him again and again as he came up to meet her, pushing up into her. She tightened around him until he felt the fire growing in the base, gathering, swelling, almost to bursting.

Waiting Cloud suddenly grimaced and let out a sharp cry. Fargo felt her shudder and contract around him as he exploded, shooting up into her, thrusting still harder, again and again. They slowed, and finally she collapsed and lay across his chest, panting.

Fargo wrapped his arms around her and held her for a long time. He heard a movement on the bed-stead and glanced over to see that Lily had just turned her back toward them. So she had watched them, Fargo realized.

After a while, Waiting Cloud got up and heated more water and they bathed silently. Waiting Cloud smiled to herself. They had just finished dressing when Fargo heard a noise outside. He grabbed his Colt and went to the window. The frost was thick on the glass, but he scraped a hole and peered out.

There was movement in the snowy woods among the dense trunks. Fargo made out several men on horseback. His grip tightened on his pistol until he spotted their buckskin wraps and long dark hair. Utes.

Waiting Cloud, looking over her shoulder, gave a cry of recognition. She threw open the door and went outside. Fargo followed. The four Indians came on silently. Riding second in line was an old man, his face dark and crinkled as a dried apple, his eyes hooded but sharp. That had to be Sitting Elk, Fargo thought.

The old chief dismounted, walked toward Waiting Cloud, and embraced her. They spoke rapidly. The three braves sat tensely on their horses. Fargo could see the anger smoldering in them as they looked off in the distance.

"My daughter," Sitting Elk began, "when I was in the white village to get the payment for our land, Blue Arrow followed us to say our summer camp was burned. I was certain you were with the Great Spirits, and my heart was empty."

Sitting Elk held his daughter at arm's length and smiled at her, then turned to Fargo.

"Beaver Man told me of you," Sitting Elk said, interest in his eyes. "We met him down by the running water. You are the one they call the Trailsman."

Fargo and Sitting Elk looked one another over in silence. He had a lot of questions for the chief. Like why Blake Griffin and his men would burn out the village. And why they would attack whites and make it look like Utes had done it. But there were certain rules of Indian etiquette that had to be followed. You couldn't just meet a chief and start asking him questions. Instead, you had to get comfortable, smoke a pipe, look one another over, share some stories. Then, and only then, could you get down to business. That was the Indian way.

"Come inside," Fargo said.

For the next hour Sitting Elk and one of his braves smoked with Fargo, while Lily sat, wide-eyed and silent, on the bedstead watching them. Waiting Cloud sat beside her father and occasionally stoked the fire. The other two braves joined McCain, who was still standing guard.

"I went to see the White Friend," the chief said at last. "In the big village."

Fargo was puzzled for a minute and then remembered that Sheriff Thomas had said that he and Sitting Elk were good friends. "You mean Sheriff Thomas?"

The chief nodded sadly.

"The White Friend has done everything he can. But the Big White Chief speaks with two tongues. And this winter my people will starve."

Sitting Elk took another puff on the pipe and passed it back to Fargo, who felt the confusion grow in him. Sheriff Thomas had done everything about what? And what White Chief was he talking about? Blake Griffin, maybe? Waiting Cloud saw the puzzlement in Fargo's face.

"Sheriff Thomas is the one in charge of the payments," Waiting Cloud piped up. "And every year they are less and less. And we are hungrier and hungrier. This year, the weak ones will die."

"What payments?" Fargo asked.

"The treaty," Sitting Elk said. "My father made a treaty with the white men who came to the valley. Once all this land was Ute land. But the white men wanted the north part. So they could dig holes in the earth."

"The gold mining," Fargo said.

"Yes. Yellow metal is too soft for arrowheads," Sitting Elk added. "Useless white man's metal. But two days ago, some of my braves found some white men digging in our hills. We told them to go and they did. But others will come."

"So, what's this payment?" Fargo asked.

"Every autumn when we move to the winter camp," Waiting Cloud explained, "the Big White Chief sends my people food. Wagonloads of food. That is the treaty payment we were promised. But every year there is less and less. And we go hungry."

"The Big White Chief in Washington has taken the land in the valley," Sitting Elk added, "but he does not send food. He said he would and he does not. The White Friend has told me he has done everything he can, but still the White Chief does not send enough food to the Utes. Down the hill, my braves wait with one wagon of food. One wagon! It is not enough. We will starve. And now my braves are angry. I have always said we must trust the White Friend and keep the peace. But now my men wish to fight."

Fargo glanced over at the young brave who sat by the fire listening to his chief. The brave's mouth was a tight, tense line and Fargo could read the smoldering hunger for revenge in his black eyes. Fargo knew that the young braves in the tribe would all be furious, having been cheated by the white men, their summer camp burned, and some of their people slaughtered.

Sitting Elk refilled the pipe and lit it again. Fargo's thoughts whirled. So Sheriff Thomas was the local Indian agent, who dispensed the shipments from Washington to pay the terms of the Utes' treaty. Fargo's thoughts went back to Martindale and he remembered when he had come riding up to the sheriff's office. There had been five mountain wagons pulling up in front of Thomas's office. And Fargo had seen the sheriff sign for them. Those loaded wagons had to be the supplies sent over Skull Pass for the Utes. But there had been five wagons, not one.

Fargo started to open his mouth to tell the chief about the other wagons he had seen, but then he shut it again. No use getting the chief riled up. Fargo realized he and McCain had to get back to Martindale fast. They had to figure out what had happened to the other four wagonloads of food for the Indians before the young braves rose up in fury. And they had to get to the bottom of the mysterious attacks.

"McCain and I were jumped, up by the long blue lake," Fargo said. "Some white men tried to make it look like Utes had done it. You have any idea why?"

Sitting Elk raised his head and gazed off into the

distance, as if looking through the walls of the cabin. "Sometimes I dream that my people are in a small tipi. The white men come, more and more of them, until my people are so close together they are touching. Then they begin to die, one by one."

"White men want all the land," Fargo said.

Sitting Elk's eyes focused on him again. "You are a wise man. You would make a good husband for my daughter."

Fargo swallowed hard.

"He is a wanderer," Waiting Cloud said, shaking her head.

"My daughter has good eyes," Sitting Elk said. He got to his feet. "Now we must take this one wagon of food from the Big White Chief and travel to the Never Winter Canyon to be hungry."

"There's some more meat outside," Fargo said. "Take that with you. Beaver Man and I got lucky yesterday. And you might send your braves over to the pond just down the hill. There's a herd of deer that comes to feed over that way."

"Many deer used to live in the valley," the Indian chief said sadly. "Now we cannot find them. Instead, there are many white men, always more and more. Like the stars in the sky."

"I might be able to help you," Fargo said, thinking of the wagons he had seen in town. "But I have to ask you to do me a favor."

"You have pleased my daughter," Sitting Elk said, a smile in his eyes.

Fargo grinned. The old chief was a sharp one. "Take the white woman with you," Skye said.

"What?" Lily shrieked from the bed. Her voice was raspy since she hadn't spoken for hours. She'd huddled in the blanket, sullen and silent. "You can't send me off with those savages! I refuse to go!"

It would serve her right, Fargo thought. And it would solve one big problem for him. He and McCain had to get back into town, but they couldn't leave Lily alone in the cabin. And taking her with them, having to guard her and keep her quiet, was out of the question.

"I will guard the white woman for Dark of Night," Waiting Cloud said, smiling slowly.

Fear crossed Lily's face.

"You'll be in good hands," Fargo said to Lily. He turned to Sitting Elk. "Meanwhile, I'll go to Martindale and find more food. Then I will come to find you."

"When you get to Martindale, the White Friend will help," Sitting Elk said. Fargo wished he had the kind of faith in Sheriff Thomas that the old chief had. The braves reappeared with extra horses and Fargo untied Lily from the bedstead.

"I can't believe you'd do this to me," she hissed, her eyes wide and afraid.

"You'll be safer with the Utes than I was in your bed," Fargo responded. "You knew all along those men were going to bust in and try to kill me. You should have told me sooner what was going on."

"I . . . I'm sorry," Lily said. "But Blake Griffin . . ."

"I'll take care of Blake," Fargo said. Lily turned

away and mounted the horse one of the braves held for her, refusing to look him in the eye. Waiting Cloud came shyly forward and put her arms around him. Fargo kissed her gently, then let her go. He noticed that Sitting Elk sat on his horse watching them, his face impassive.

The Indians moved off through the snowy woods. Just as they were nearly out of sight, Fargo saw another figure appear, heading toward him. It was McCain on snowshoes.

"We've got to get back to town," Fargo said.

"Yeah. I spotted some men from Martindale over the next rise," McCain said. "They're looking for us for sure."

Fargo thought for a minute and then had an idea. They went back inside and hunted about the small cabin, soon finding what they needed. Some old prospectors' clothes, dusty and battered, hung on some pegs, and two beaten-up hats were under the beds. Fargo found a rusty razor in a drawer of the washstand and he quickly stropped it and shaved with soapsuds. As McCain shaved, Fargo toweled his face dry and peered into the dim, cracked mirror that hung behind the door. Without their beards, wearing wide-brimmed hats pulled low and battered clothes, and with pickaxes over their shoulders, nobody in Martindale would take notice of them. They would just blend into the crowd of desperate gold seekers. That was exactly the idea.

By noon, Fargo and McCain were saddled up, their regular clothes packed into their saddlebags.

They looked like two gold hunters for sure, Fargo thought, their saddles loaded down with pans and pickaxes.

The horses picked their way through the trees and down the hill toward the trail that led back to town. They had gone only a mile and were riding side by side across a bare white meadow when Fargo sensed trouble. He glanced sideways at McCain and then spotted movement in the fringe of trees at the edge of the clearing. Suddenly a shot rang out and echoed through the still air. Ten men on horseback broke out of the trees on all sides of them and raced forward in a line. For a moment, Fargo considered running, but quickly realized they were surrounded. They'd have to bluff their way out.

"I'll do the talking," he said to McCain quietly. They both pulled their hats low and adjusted their collars up high, as if against the cold. The less of their faces that showed, the better.

The men, their saddles and bridles creaking in the still air, encircled them. Burly Joe, his brown beard icy where his steaming breath had frozen, was in the lead.

"What's the trouble?" Fargo asked, his voice friendly.

"We're looking for a kidnapper," Burly Joe said. "Took a lady dove from Martindale. Big, tall fellow."

" 'Bout my size?" Fargo asked nonchalantly.

"Bigger," Burly Joe said. "You seen him?"

"Ain't seen anybody running around with a

painted woman out here," Fargo answered. "Wish I had. We've been up in that miners' cabin." Fargo wanted to mention that so that when Burly Joe and his men stopped by there and found it had been occupied, their suspicions wouldn't be further aroused. "But now we're going to head into town and get a piece of that gold action up in the hills."

"You do that," Burly Joe said with a smile. "And watch out. Those goddamn Utes have gone on the warpath."

"What?" Fargo asked.

"They've all gone crazy," Burly Joe answered. "Killing everybody in sight. Just ride with your guns ready."

"Thanks for the warning," Fargo said.

The men pulled their horses around and sped off, disappearing into the woods. Fargo felt the confusion sweep over him. The Utes couldn't have attacked already. They had seen Sitting Elk barely an hour before, and although he had hinted that his braves were angry and ready for revenge, it was impossible that the fighting had broken out already.

The clouds, still low and filled with snow, hid the tops of the peaks, and the dark, forested mountainsides were deeply sugared with snow. Soon they were sitting on their horses at the top of the hill, overlooking the town. Below, a crowd of men gathered at the edge of town. He and McCain rode slowly down the hill, coming up behind the crowd. Even on horseback, it was impossible to see over the men's heads to get a glimpse at what was causing the ruckus. Fargo and McCain dismounted and pushed their way through the muttering, angry men. In a few moments, they had worked their way to the front.

There, lying face up, was the body of Jake Keenan. Beside him lay the other man Fargo had shot in the attack by the lake. Both of the men had tomahawks driven into their skulls and several arrows protruding from their bellies. Their scalps had been lifted and their skulls were black with dried blood.

Tacked to a tree trunk over the bodies was a huge, hand-lettered sign that read: UTES DONE THIS.

5

"Goddamn redskins," one man muttered, looking down at the corpses.

"We oughtta kill those savages before they get us," another said.

"I hear there's a big meeting at four o'clock in the hotel bar," another added. "We're going to do something about this."

McCain's silver-flecked eyebrows shot up as he caught Fargo's glance. The two of them made their way back through the crowd toward their horses. Fargo and McCain had left the bodies of the two men back at the lake with bullets in them. For a moment, Fargo considered the possibility that wandering Utes had come on the dead men and had mutilated them, but he knew it wasn't true. No Indian warrior would ever lift the scalp of a man he hadn't killed himself. So it must be that Blake Griffin's men had found the bodies of Jake and the other man, had scalped them, plugged them with arrows, and hauled them back to Martindale, just to get everybody riled up against the Utes. And it had worked. The men in the crowd were angry and ready to go shoot up the Indians.

Fargo's thoughts went back to Sheriff Thomas and the conversation they'd had. Thomas had seemed genuinely concerned about the Utes and the attacks. And Sitting Elk had called him the White Friend. The sheriff had promised he was going to get to the bottom of all this, but Fargo had his suspicions. More than anything, he wanted to have a talk with the sheriff and find out once and for all just where he stood.

Fargo and McCain rode through the snow-choked streets of Martindale, their horses stuttering on the choppy, frozen mud beneath the layer of dirty snow. The sheriff's office came into view, and Fargo dismounted and crossed to the door while McCain waited outside with instructions to come in after him in ten minutes if he didn't reappear.

A deputy sat reading the paper inside the office, his feet on the desk.

"Sheriff Thomas around?" Fargo asked.

The deputy glanced up, took in Fargo's tattered clothes and wide prospector's hat, and looked down again. "He's around."

Fargo waited for a moment, feeling his anger grow. "Where is he?" he growled.

The deputy started and shot him a defiant look. "He's busy at the moment," the deputy said. "Or ain't you heard? We got trouble in the town. You need something?"

"When's Sheriff Thomas due back?"

"Check in a couple hours," the deputy said. "What's your name? I'll tell him you stopped by."

"I'll come back later," Fargo said, beating a hasty retreat. There was no need to let the sheriff know he was poking around Martindale again. Especially if the sheriff was up to no good.

Fargo mounted the roan again and he and McCain rode down the street slowly. They just didn't seem to be getting anywhere. How the hell could he pin the attacks on Blake Griffin?

His thoughts turned to the missing Ovaro and he felt a sense of hopelessness settle on him. Would he ever find the faithful pinto again? Whoever had stolen his horse might be halfway to Kansas by now, if they'd taken the horse across the pass.

"We've got a couple of hours to kill," Fargo said to McCain. "What would two prospectors do?"

"Go drinking maybe?" McCain said with a grin.

"I don't relish hanging around the Martindale Hotel again," Fargo said. "Besides, we'll get over there at four o'clock for the big meeting. Without our beards and in the middle of the crowd, I doubt anyone will recognize us. Got another idea?"

"Let's go look at that land-claim office," McCain said.

The two of them rode the short distance to the office and tethered their horses outside. With all the excitement generated by the corpses on display, there was nobody around. They walked into a bare room with a mud-spattered floor and a big wooden counter. On one wall hung a detailed map of the big valley with mining claims marked on it. Tacked to the other wall were newspaper accounts of the fabulous gold strikes that had occurred in the valley during the last few years. *Nugget big as a walnut found on the ground* one account read. Another told the story of a man from Virginia who rented a claim and within the first hour dug up three pokefuls of high-grade gold—three thousand dollars worth for an hour's work. There were dozens more newspaper stories, all telling the same got-rich-quick story. McCain and Fargo were reading the clippings when a door opened behind the counter and a spidery-looking kid emerged. His face brightened when he looked them over.

"You fellows looking to rent a gold claim?" he asked, running a skinny hand through his dark hair. "We got some of the best gold fields in the whole world. Why, hundreds of men have come through here and made their fortunes."

"So it seems," Fargo said. "But how come the owners don't mine the gold themselves?"

The kid's eyes shifted from Fargo to McCain but he didn't hesitate a moment. "Those guys are rich," the kid said conspiratorially. "They don't want to get their hands dirty with gold mining. They're just as happy to share the wealth, let somebody else get it out of the ground. Besides, they've got more money than they need already."

Fargo let his eyes wander over the map as he thought over the kid's words. From what he'd seen of rich men, they never had enough money. Once they got rich, they just wanted more and more.

And the speech the kid had given them sounded rehearsed, like he'd recited it to every gold-hungry fool who'd ever walked in the door.

"Sounds interesting," Fargo said, trying to appear gullible. "So, what's the deal?"

The kid gave a broad smile, like an eager fisherman who suddenly got a tug on his line. "I got just the thing for you," he said, walking over to the map. He pointed at a spot on the saddle between two hills. "This place is prime. Got a stream, and there's already a Long Tom set up there for washing the rocks. Last guy who rented it made a half-million bucks."

"So why didn't he keep mining?" Fargo asked.

The kid shifted from foot to foot. "He . . . got hitched to some broad who wanted to go back East," the kid said. "He didn't want to go. He wanted to stay and make a full million. He left town just this morning, and if you don't take this piece, somebody else is bound to."

"So, how much does it rent for?" Fargo asked.

The kid put up his hands. "Not so fast," he said. "I wouldn't talk money with you until you've had a chance to go up there and inspect it. It's a ten-minute ride up the hill. Once you take a look at it, then we can talk price.

Fargo and McCain exchanged looks. The kid was a damned smooth salesman, Fargo thought. They had nothing to do for the next two hours anyway, so why not? McCain nodded almost imperceptibly.

"Sure," Fargo said. "Let's go see the property.

The kid came around from the back of the land office riding a swaybacked gray. The three of them rode slowly up the main street and took the trail leading toward the goldfields. The mountainside above the town was littered with scree and the mine tailings from dozens of excavations. Past the town limit, where the trail turned upward, they spotted a couple of prospectors squatting by the half-frozen stream, panning. The wind blew hard, pushing the snow into drifts and exposing some of the rocks which lay beneath.

The horses picked their way up the steep grade slowly, plodding up the switchbacks until the rocky, snowbound trail suddenly leveled. Water bubbled in a dark stream that tumbled down the hillside. There were footprints all around and a place where the snow had been cleared from the yellow-orange rocks. Somebody had been digging in the face of the mountainside.

They all dismounted. "See," the kid said, advancing on the cleared spot. "Now, the guy who had this claim before had a real nose for gold. I mean, he'd already found a half-million dollars worth. And he swore up and down there was a mother lode right under this rock. But that woman he married just didn't want to wait any longer for him to find it." The kid shrugged and walked nonchalantly back to his horse. "You look around all you want," he offered. "Maybe have a dig or two in the ground. See what you think of this parcel. I have to go check on somebody down this way and

I'll come back for you in about ten minutes." The kid mounted and was soon out of sight.

"What do you think the game is?" McCain said.

"I'm not sure," Fargo said. "But if we were really prospectors, we'd take our pickaxes to some rock and see what we could find."

McCain agreed and they pulled the picks from their saddlebags and started on the cleared rock. Fargo chipped away at a solid face of orange rock while McCain struck at another section for a while, the rhythmic ringing of their picks echoing off the rocks above. Then Fargo saw a glitter and he shifted his aim toward it. The tip of the pick sank deep into the rock and he pulled back hard on the handle. Rock tumbled away and he spotted color. Gold!

"Hey," Fargo said, motioning to McCain.

McCain rested his pick on the ground and came over. The two of them knelt and began picking through the shattered rock.

"Hell," the trapper said, "there *is* a lot of gold in this rock."

Fargo picked up the golden bits from among the rock and put them on his open palm. He continued sorting through the rocks to gather the small nuggets and gold shot until he couldn't find any more. He stood and looked down at the fistful of gold.

"That's at least two hundred dollars worth," McCain said in amazement. "A damned good month's wages for most men."

Fargo nodded, looking from the gold in his palm

to the ground and back again. What was going on? They heard the sound of the kid approaching and he soon appeared around the corner, drawing up his horse and dismounting.

"Find anything?" the kid asked.

"Sure did," Fargo said, playing the part of an amazed prospector who was trying to remain calm. "Found a whole bunch of it." He showed the kid what he had in his hand. The kid whistled.

"So, I guess that guy was right about that mother lode," the kid said. "There's probably two million bucks right there under that rock, just waiting to be taken out."

"Now, how much is the rent on this land?" Fargo asked.

"We'd sure like to be millionaires," McCain put in, tugging on his hat.

"It's only two thousand dollars for three months. In advance," the kid said quickly, and then added in a serious tone. "You got that kind of money?"

"Oh, sure," Fargo said diffidently. "We think of it as an investment."

"That's right!" the kid said. "It's a bargain. And I'll tell you what." He leaned in close and winked at them. "Legally, that gold belongs to the company, since you ain't rented the land yet. But you look like nice fellows. So just to clinch the deal, I'll count that as your down payment. We'll take it back to the office and weigh it—looks like a couple hundred bucks worth to me. So that's ten percent off the rental price. Not bad for a few minutes' work."

The kid babbled on as Fargo turned the gold over to him. He stowed it in an empty leather poke he took out of his pocket. All the way back to town, the kid talked about how rich they would be, how lucky they were to grab this choice claim just when that other guy had gone back East, and calculating how much money they could make if they'd found a couple hundred dollars worth of gold in just ten minutes.

When they arrived back at the office, the kid disappeared behind the building to tether his horse while Fargo and McCain tied theirs up out in front. "This is damned fishy," Fargo said. "And I think I know what's going on. But I want to take a look in that back room. You get the kid out front for a few minutes and I'll slip in there."

McCain agreed and they entered the office. The kid appeared at the door behind the counter and threw the poke down on the counter. He rubbed his hands together in delight.

"You fellows are real lucky. Real lucky. Why, in three months, you'll have more gold than you know what to do with."

"Sounds good to me," McCain said. "I'm going to get that rent money out of my saddlebags, but I could use some help. Come out with me."

Fargo stared at the map, ignoring McCain who was speaking directly to the kid. The kid took the bait. "Sure," he said, clapping McCain on the shoulder. They went out the door and Fargo moved swiftly behind the counter. As he opened the back door, he glanced through the window and saw Mc-

Cain take a tumble on the boardwalk outside. The kid leaned down to help him up. The old trapper would keep the kid distracted, Fargo knew.

The back room was a kind of storeroom filled with rifles and crates and a potbellied stove in one corner. Stacked on one table were bullet molds and small boxes of ammunition. He picked up one and opened it. Inside were golden bullets. He whistled low and smiled to himself. It was just as he had suspected. The Martindale Land Leasing Company was salting the claims.

Fargo removed his hat and absently loaded a Henry rifle with a couple of the gold bullets as his thoughts stirred. Salting claims was an old trick in the West. You scattered some gold shot on the ground and then brought in a couple of tenderfoot prospectors who spotted the gold and bought the land at top dollar. Or, better yet, you loaded some rifles with golden bullets and shot them into the rock. When the chumps dug the bullets out, the gold had splintered against the rock and looked pretty natural. So, that was the game.

Just then, Fargo heard footsteps—not from the front office but at the back door. The latch clicked and Fargo whirled about, bringing the Henry rifle up before him. The door swung open. Blake Griffin stood there.

The tiny man wore a light-brown suit and a red silk vest with a gigantic gold watch chain across it, which only made him look all the more dwarfish. His deep, hooded eyes registered mild surprise to see Fargo standing there with a Henry pointed straight at his chest.

"Close the door behind you," Fargo said quietly. "Or else."

Griffin smiled coldly, looking down the length of the gun. "Or else what?" he asked.

"I salt you with some of your own gold," Fargo answered.

Blake did as he was told, his piercing eyes never leaving Fargo's. "And who might you be?" Griffin asked. "A failed gold miner perhaps? Someone on whom Lady Luck has not smiled?" The small man reached inside his front jacket pocket.

"Freeze," Fargo said. "Take that hand out slowly or you'll lose it." Griffin smiled and withdrew his hand, which now held a fat cigar.

"May I smoke?" the little man asked. He started to reach into his picket again and then stopped. He wrenched one end off the cigar and then moved cautiously, holding his hands carefully away from his sides, toward the potbellied stove, where he opened the small door below and lit his cigar.

"I know your game, Griffin," Fargo said.

"Such a rare pleasure to meet a smart man," Griffin answered. "But you have an advantage over me. I don't even know your name."

"Yes you do," Fargo said quietly. He was beginning to wonder what had happened to McCain and the kid. The old trapper could keep the kid occupied for only so long. And when they came back into the office and discovered Fargo was not there, the kid would come looking in the back room.

Blake Griffin regarded him for a long moment. "Oh," he said, sounding almost pleased. "You're the famous *Mr. Fargo*. I should have known. But I thought you'd escaped over Skull Pass with the darling Miss Lily. How is she, by the way?"

"She's fine," Fargo snapped. Where the hell was McCain anyway? he wondered. He didn't hear a sound from the front room.

"Oh, Miss Lily probably didn't take very well to being kidnapped. Where is she anyway?" Griffin asked, flicking the ash of his cigar onto the floor.

"Enough chatter," Fargo said.

Just then, the door to the outer room opened behind him. Fargo heard the click of a pistol. He whirled about to see Burly Joe standing there, his small eyes glaring down the very long barrel of a Colt Navy, which was pointed straight at Fargo.

"Drop the rifle," Blake Griffin said. "And the pistol. I got you covered too." Two more men piled behind Burly Joe, their big pistols drawn.

Fargo glanced around to see the compact Dimick derringer that had materialized in Blake Griffin's hand. For a moment, Fargo considered a shoot-out, four against one. But then he realized he didn't have a chance. Fargo reluctantly dropped the rifle onto the floor and then stripped off his gun belt.

"Kick them over here," Burly Joe growled. Fargo did so. He wondered where McCain had got to, and if Burly Joe hadn't run into him in on his way into the land-leasing office.

"Well, Mr. Fargo," Blake Griffin said, relighting

his cigar at the stove with one hand while maintaining a grip on his Dimick with the other. He puffed the cigar furiously for a moment and then removed it from his mouth. "You made a terrible mess at the hotel the other night. Scared all the girls. We don't like that kind of behavior in such a law-abiding town."

There was a noise out back. The door opened and a big man with a mustache came in, collaring McCain. He threw him roughly down on the floor. "Oh, good evening, Mr. Griffin, sir," the mustachioed man said obsequiously. "I found this scum lurking outside. He'd knocked out Eddie, and when he saw me coming, he yelled something about my mustache. So I got him. I guess he was going to rob the place."

It was clear the man was not very bright, Fargo thought. He caught McCain's glance and knew that the old trapper had recognized the man who had been one of the attackers at the lake. But the mustachioed man clearly hadn't recognized them.

Griffin looked over Fargo and McCain. "These are clever boys," Griffin said. "Very clever. And dangerous. You and Burly Joe will stay here and keep a good eye on them, won't you?"

"Sure boss," the mustachioed man said hastily. Blake Griffin drew a large watch out of his pocket and consulted it. Fargo looked around. Griffin was obviously intending to leave him and McCain there with the two guards. Two against two. Fargo liked the odds and his mind began to search for ways to get free. He and McCain would be tied up for certain. But he had the knife strapped to his ankle. They'd distract the two men somehow. As he covertly surveyed the room for anything that might give them an advantage, he felt hope rise in him.

"Almost time for the board meeting," Blake Griffin said thoughtfully. He glanced sharply at Fargo and caught the direction of his gaze. Suspicion filled Griffin's face. "On second thought," he said, "you boys bring them along to the hotel. I'd like to keep an eye on them myself."

Fargo swore silently to himself as the big men approached. This was not going well. He sized up the four men and shot a look at McCain, who signaled by blinking his eyes once. Yeah, they'd try to fight it out. Bad odds, but it was better than being trussed up and taken as a display for Griffin's Gold Club. The mustachioed man took hold of McCain's arm while another approached Fargo, uncoiling a length of rope. Blake Griffin snipped the end off a fresh cigar while Burly Joe stood aside, covering them with his long Colt Navy.

When the man grabbed Fargo's arm, he swung around, kneed the man in the groin, and then followed with a swift uppercut that left the man slumped on the floor, groaning. Burly Joe shouted and waved his Colt while McCain swung at the man with the mustache. The other one hurtled toward Fargo, who stuck out his foot at the last moment, then stepped aside so that the man went down, hard, crashing against a table and splintering it. A shot rang out and McCain stifled a yell. Fargo saw the old trapper holding one arm.

"The next one's through the heart," Griffin said, his eyes cold as a viper's above the smoking snub barrel of his Dimick derringer. The mustachioed man got up groaning from the floor. The other two men were out cold.

"Tie them up," Griffin barked. "Tight. I told you they were dangerous."

Fargo didn't try anything else. One look at the dwarf told him that a single move would get him a bullet. And he had no doubt the ice-eyed man was a sure shot.

In moments, Griffin's men had bound their hands behind their backs and gagged them. The other two men regained consciousness and staggered to their feet, wiping the blood off their faces and shooting angry looks at Fargo. The four big men crowded around Fargo and McCain, and with Griffin in the lead, hustled them out the back door and into the snowy alleyway.

They went several short blocks, staying off the main thoroughfares, until they came to a side entrance of the Martindale Hotel. Griffin rapped the door sharply, two fast taps and a pause followed by two more, and the door opened slowly. They were pushed inside and Fargo found himself in a small hallway. As they were moving along it, a side door opened and Fargo glanced in to see the dark girl in the ivory dress. He winked at her above his gag and she registered puzzlement, then shock, when she recognized him without his beard. She hastily closed the door after he passed by. Griffin instructed his men to leave Fargo's and McCain's gun belts hanging on pegs on the wall. The hallway led to a small door, concealed beneath red velvet draperies, which led into the back of the Gold Club.

Blake Griffin motioned Burly Joe to bind Fargo and McCain to two chairs along the side where he could keep an eye on them. The big, bearded man used a lot of rope tying them up, and Griffin checked the knots afterward and asked that they be tightened. Then he dismissed the four men, asking them to stand outside, ready if he needed them. The roar and clatter of the bar crowd in the big room next door filtered underneath the door. Fargo and McCain, gagged and bound tight to the chairs, looked around the red-velvet-draped room with its big table and low-hanging gas lamp.

Blake Griffin ignored them. He seated himself at the head of the table on a special chair that Fargo noticed was built very high. Then he lit a cigar and bent over a sheaf of papers, turning them one by one. Fargo grew restless and his mind began to plan ways of escape. He reached for the throwing knife, straining against the ropes but there was no give. Not even half an inch. No way could he reach his ankle holster and get the knife. Teeth? He wondered. He bent his head down and looked at the thick cords crossing his chest. Nope, not unless he had steel incisors and all night to chew. He tightened his thighs and tested whether he could get up and stagger a few feet with the chair tied to him. But, he asked himself, what good would that do? Blake Griffin's Dimick would plug him before he stumbled a yard.

No, escape was impossible. So instead Fargo concentrated his gaze and his mind on Blake Griffin. He wondered what the connection was with Washington and with Blake's brother, Senator Joshua Griffin. Griffin was behind the attacks on the Utes. And behind the salting of the gold mines. But what was it all about? What was the connection?

Griffin slowly raised his eyes from the paper he was studying. Without looking at Fargo, he spoke in a monotone. "You'll find out everything you want to know, Mr. Fargo. All in due time." Then Griffin looked down at his paper again. Fargo felt the hair prickle on the back of his neck, and for one moment he wondered if the dwarf could read his mind.

After a few moments, the door to the bar opened. The sound of talking, laughter, and some out-of-tune piano music drifted into the room on a sudden swell as a few men in fine linen suits came in. They closed the door behind them and looked startled to see Fargo and McCain tied to chairs. Griffin, without rising, motioned them to take a seat.

"Never mind them," Griffin said. "Some special guests. I'll explain later." In another five minutes, the chairs were filled. Fargo studied each of the men in the room. They were all well-heeled businessmen, and the room fairly glittered with the arcs of heavy gold watch chains and diamond stickpins. Griffin looked up again from his papers.

"The Board of Directors is assembled," he said, looking around at the other men. "This meeting is called to order. Now the first order of business is the financial report."

A portly man in a blue suit rose, adjusted his spectacles, and cleared his throat. "Can we talk in front of those two?" he asked nervously, nodding toward Fargo and McCain.

"Ah, yes. Let me introduce you to our guests. This is the famous Skye Fargo and his sidekick," Griffin answered.

The men gathered around the table turned and looked at them with curiosity. Fargo thought of a dozen nasty comments he would like to make back to them and silently cursed the gag tight across his mouth.

"Mr. Fargo's the one who caused all the trouble here the other night," Griffin added. "And this afternoon he was poking around in the back room of the land office. Given the circumstances, my boys will take care of them right after this meeting. So it doesn't matter what they hear."

"Well then," the man continued, turning back to the table, "according to our books, The Martindale Land Leasing Company has just reached our goal of two hundred and fifty thousand dollars. The money's set aside, minus expenses," he said. He glanced over his spectacles and added, "And minus payments to the board, of course." A chuckle went around the room.

"Fine, fine," Blake Griffin said. "That means we have enough money for me to deliver to Washington." Fargo's ears perked up. Now he would hear about that deal with Washington which probably involved Griffin's brother, the senator.

"Now just what kind of guarantee have we got on this thing?" asked an elderly man with a large, gray, handlebar mustache. "I mean, can Joshua Griffin guarantee that they'll vote the way we want?"

Fargo strained against the ropes, listening intently.

"Good question," Griffin said. "My brother's got a lot of power among his fellow senators. Half of this money will be used to buy the few necessary votes. And with the rest we'll buy the whole south end of the valley . . . once the U.S. government nullifies the treaty with the Utes."

So that was it, Fargo thought, exchanging looks with McCain. The whole thing was just a high-stakes land grab, with Blake Griffin and his Gold Club aiming to take over the whole valley with the help of some crooked senators. Hell, they'd do it too.

"The Senate is sure to vote our way once I take them word of these Ute attacks," Griffin continued. "Meanwhile, everything is ready for the meeting at four o'clock, directly following this one. Burly Joe is going to get the men stirred up and organized against the Indians. After tonight, there'll be plenty of whites dead. We'll send the newspaper reports straight to Washington and that will help the vote along."

The men around the table nodded agreement and muttered to one another. It was a diabolical plan, Fargo thought. But it would work, damn it.

"Now we'll hear from Mr. Perkins about the survey," Griffin announced.

A tall, silver-haired man rose and grasped his lapel with one hand. "As you know," he said, "I hired a couple of prospectors last week to travel down into Ute land to dig a little. Look around for color. Well, it's just like we always suspected. There's no gold in that land, but plenty of quartz. Now, gold hunters always look for quartz, which is where most gold strikes occur. So with some careful salting, that land will look like El Dorado."

"And with that land, we can reinvigorate interest in this valley," Griffin said.

"The two prospectors got back to town and reported to me," the silver-haired man added. "Then they started to ask questions. I had them taken care of."

"Good," Griffin nodded. "We don't want any leaks. It would be a disaster for all of us if anyone knew there's no gold in this whole valley. This land would be completely worthless and we'd all go broke. But when we open up that Ute land and stage a few strikes, word will get around and we'll have more suckers pouring into Martindale than we have land to rent to them. That will drive prices sky-high."

"Sounds good to me," a pale man said, and Fargo

recognized the shopkeeper who had wanted to charge him a hundred and forty dollars for supplies. So the store owners were in on it too, he realized. Sure. If the Martindale Land Leasing Company attracted hundreds more prospectors to the valley, they could drive the price of goods even higher. Everybody would get rich except for the suckers, the gold-hungry prospectors who poured into town.

The noise from the bar had increased, and through the door Fargo could hear men shouting. Griffin noticed the noise too. "It's time for the big meeting," he said. "Let's go." Griffin jumped down from the tall chair and headed for the door. Just as he passed Fargo, he paused. "I hope your curiosity is finally satisfied, Mr. Fargo," he said. "Too bad it won't do you any good. This meeting will last ten minutes. And then I'll return and have you shot."

The room cleared and the door was pulled partially shut. It remained open a crack, so Fargo and McCain were able to hear what was going on in the bar. Fargo looked bleakly at McCain, his thoughts racing again on how they might escape. The ropes were too tight for him to reach the knife strapped on his ankle. Once again, he tightened the powerful muscles of his thighs. Yes, if he rocked the chair forward a few times, he might just be able to propel himself onto his feet. And then what? He glanced around the room and noticed a water glass on the table. Glass. If he could knock it onto the floor and shatter it, then tip over and rub

the ropes against the sharp edge . . . maybe
. . . maybe. It was a long shot for sure.

Fargo glanced at the clock on the wall. Five minutes after four. Griffin had said ten minutes. Fargo
turned his head and looked at McCain. Using his
eyes, he glanced toward the table and the water
glass. McCain raised his brows in puzzlement.
Goddamn these gags, Fargo thought. Finally, Mc-
Cain nodded slowly. Maybe he understood what
the plan was, Fargo thought.

He hunched his shoulders forward and began
rocking the chair, slowly at first and then in greater
arcs until he could inch it bit by bit away from the
wall. Then, with one final swing, he came forward
and landed on his feet, standing crouched over
with the chair tied tight from his upper body all the
way down to his shins.

Fargo moved forward, shuffling his feet along
the floor as he approached the table. He came
nearer and nearer, the water glass shimmering like
diamonds in the gaslight. He was only a foot away
from the table when he thought he heard the door
creak. Someone was about to enter the room.
There was no time to get the chair back into
place. Fargo froze and then decided to sit back
down in the chair. He threw his weight backward
and the chair legs came back to the ground. Then
Fargo heard wood splinter as one of the legs shattered and the chair pitched sideways. He toppled
over and lay on his side, tied tight to the chair,
helpless and defeated.

Fargo silently swore every curse he could think

of—and then some. Now he was as stuck as a turtle on its back. It was absolutely impossible to move or to do anything at all. He couldn't see McCain, but he could see the clock on the wall. It was now ten minutes after four. They had five minutes until Griffin came back to kill them.

Behind him, Fargo heard McCain start to rock his chair. Having seen what Fargo was attempting, McCain was going to try the same trick. The rhythmic beat of the chair legs hitting the wooden floor accelerated and then Fargo heard a crash. The old trapper had gone over in his chair, too. Hell, Griffin would come back in and find them lying on the floor like two trussed birds. And the dwarf would get great delight in seeing how their attempts at escape had come to nothing.

Fargo's mind continued to try possibilities. Roll against the table, maybe the water glass would fall onto the floor? But he couldn't move even a foot toward the table leg. Reach up with his head and pull the tablecloth with his teeth? No way. The edge of the cloth was a good foot above him, well out of reach.

The minute hand moved into horizontal position. It was four-fifteen. Fargo heard a door open and light footsteps approach. In his despair, it took him a moment to realize that it was not the door to the bar which had opened, but the one hidden behind the draperies which led to the back hallway. Just then, he felt a hand laid on his shoulder and smelled lemon verbena. He knew it was the dark woman in the ivory dress, although she knelt behind him and he could not see her face. He felt the ropes binding him being sliced apart. The bonds loosened. She worked fast, but Fargo could sense she was nervous. In a moment, his arms came free and he reached around with an open hand. She pressed the knife into it and he quickly sliced the other ropes.

The clock read four-seventeen. At any moment Griffin would reenter the room. From the bar came the shouts and calls of men angry and ready to fight. Fargo rolled away from the chair, disentangling himself from the cut ropes. He tore the gag from his mouth and glanced at the woman. "Thanks," he said. "Get back in the hallway before Griffin comes back." She would die with them if they were discovered. The woman smiled and disappeared through the door.

Fargo bent over McCain and had him nearly free when he heard the doorknob jiggle. Fargo swore to himself. Just one more minute, he thought, and they'd be free. The door creaked open as he continued slicing the ropes from McCain. Sounds from the bar wafted into the room and Fargo looked up to see Blake Griffin's small form just outside the half-opened door. His back was turned and he was talking to someone. At any moment he would turn and enter the room. Fargo almost had McCain free. Griffin still had not turned. Fargo sliced through the last of the ropes and pulled the old trapper to his feet. They hastily strode across the room to the small door hidden by the draperies, Fargo expecting to get a bullet in his back at any moment. But they made it through the door and scampered down the hallway. Fargo knew that Griffin would raise the alarm momentarily. They had just seconds to spare. He'd grabbed his holster and Colt as he passed. The woman in the ivory dress was nowhere in sight. Fargo fleetingly wished he could have thanked her properly, but there was no time.

"Out the back!" Fargo exclaimed, buckling on his gun belt as McCain did the same. They stumbled out of the door and Fargo led the way through the trampled snow toward the dark stables. Griffin would expect them to steal horses and ride out. He'd be looking for men on horseback. They entered the stable, leaving the double doors open behind them, and Fargo let a few of the horses out of their stalls, driving them out the doors with a sharp slap. Then he and McCain ran the length of the long, dark shed, exiting out the far end through a door Fargo had noticed the night he'd kidnapped Lily. They found themselves on a narrow back street. Fargo glanced both ways and then spotted one edge of the sheriff's office around the corner.

Sheriff Thomas. Was he in on this deal of Blake Griffin's or not? He was a friend of Sitting Elk's, after all. The chief trusted Thomas completely. But there was also the matter of the missing supply wagons. After a moment's thought, Fargo decided to head for the sheriff's office. A jailhouse would be the last place Griffin would think to look for them. Fargo could get some questions answered, and maybe get some help. Behind them, from the direction of the hotel, Fargo heard no noise. What the hell was taking Griffin so long? Where was the alarm anyway?

They sprinted across the deserted street and climbed the steps onto the boardwalk. Fargo glanced through the window to see that the office was deserted. The door was locked. He swore to himself, then pulled the Arkansas toothpick from his ankle holster and jimmied the lock with the sharp tip of the knife. He and McCain swiftly entered and locked the door behind them. Fargo drew the shades in case anybody glanced in.

"Close call," McCain said, rubbing his wrists where the ropes had cut into them. "You always live this dangerously?"

"Sure," Fargo said with a grin. "Now we wait for the sheriff. I got to find out if he's straight or not. He seems like he's on Sitting Elk's side. And we need an ally right now."

Fargo eased himself down onto Sheriff Thomas's desk, which was piled high with papers in folders. A tall stack slid to the floor and papers scattered everywhere.

"Oh, hell," Fargo said, and bent to retrieve them. He was stuffing documents back into the folders when something caught his eye. It was a form, with the seal of the U.S. government on the top. Underneath was written "Form 9574, Requisition for Supplies in Compliance with Treaty Number 124, Ute Tribe, Colorado Territory."

Fargo scanned the paper, reading the list of supplies noted: seventy-five crates of dried beef, fifty-five barrels of wheat flour, forty of cornmeal, and so on. It was dated three years earlier and bore Sheriff Thomas's signature. Fargo rifled through the papers, finding more of the documents and looking for the one he had seen the sheriff sign two days before. Finally he spotted it and read it quickly. It specified the same quantities, starting with the seventy-five crates of dried beef. At the bottom, by his signature, Thomas had written "Five wagonloads received."

McCain looked up from gathering papers from the floor when Fargo gave a low whistle. "What you got?" the trapper asked.

"Evidence," Fargo said, gathering the last few years' receipts and stuffing them inside his shirt. He had his mouth open to tell McCain that Sheriff Thomas was cheating his old friends the Utes when he sensed a whisper of movement outside the office.

His Colt was out of its holster in a flash as a heavy body crashed against the door and it stove in, splintering in all directions. At the same moment two men crashed through the windows. They landed on the floor and rolled onto their sides, guns blazing. In an instant the air was filled with whining bullets, which poured through the broken door and the shattered windowpanes. Fargo plugged one of the men in the chest and McCain coldcocked the other before he could get to his feet.

Then the old trapper cried out and slumped to the floor. He'd been hit. Fargo dashed forward among the whizzing bullets and pulled McCain around to the back of the heavy wooden desk, which shielded them from the fusillade.

"I took one in the stomach," McCain gasped. "God almighty, I'm not sure I'm going to make it." The old trapper's face was pale, but his eyes blazed with defiance. Fargo took a look at the wound. McCain might pull through if he could get a doctor's attention immediately. Fargo propped him up against the desk. Just then, the gunfire ceased.

"Give up, Fargo. Toss your guns out where we can see them and get your hands up," a voice called out. "We got the whole building surrounded. You haven't got a chance."

Fargo swore to himself.

The voice was unmistakable. It was Sheriff Thomas.

6

Fargo hesitated for a moment as the guns went silent. They were surrounded. Probably a hundred armed men stood poised to shoot the hell out of them if they stuck a toe out the front door. And Fargo's last hope, that Sheriff Thomas would be an ally, was dashed. Thomas was not only cheating the Utes out of their winter supplies, but he was right in the middle of Blake Griffin's web of deceit. He and McCain didn't have a snowball's chance in hell.

For a moment, Fargo considered shooting out the big gas lamp in the office. Then he could see better into the darkness of the street and they wouldn't be such sitting ducks. He eyed the flickering lamp hanging in the corner, but immediately realized that the fallen lamp would start a fire. They could either roast or face the flying lead.

Fargo took another look at McCain's wound. His only hope was to get to a doctor. But expecting the old trapper to dash out of the sheriff's office through flying bullets while bleeding from the stomach? Well, that would kill him for sure.

"Forget about me," McCain said. "You get out of here."

"Well?" Thomas shouted in the silence. "What's your answer? You giving up?" Fargo realized if he tried to escape, things would only go worse for McCain.

"Yeah!" Fargo shouted back. "Yeah, we're giving up. But first I want to talk to Griffin. And Thomas."

"What've you got in mind?" McCain whispered.

"Staying alive," Fargo replied. "I'm going to try to talk Griffin into hiring me."

"What?" McCain asked, shocked.

"Okay!" Thomas shouted back. "Throw your weapons out the front window and get your hands over your heads."

Fargo got their two pistols and threw them out of the shattered window.

"You trust those bastards?" the old trapper asked, shaking his head.

"We don't have any other choice," Fargo said grimly. It was the biggest chance he'd ever taken, facing unarmed the wily Blake Griffin and the dishonest sheriff. But there was no choice. He knew that he couldn't hold off all the men of Martindale. Fargo slowly stood up, arms over his head, muscles tense, ready for the gunfire to start up again.

"Hold your fire!" Thomas shouted. "Stand in front of the window where we can see you. Where's the old man?"

"Shot up! Lying on the floor. Where's Griffin?" Fargo shouted.

133

Just then he spotted the short man striding forward, Dimick in hand, across the icy street, followed by Sheriff Thomas, Burly Joe, and three other men, all with pistols at the ready. They weren't taking any chances. One false move and he was a dead man. Griffin kept his eyes locked on Fargo as he walked slowly up the steps. Burly Joe was first to enter the office through the battered door. He crossed the room quickly, looked down at the wounded McCain, and then waved his pistol at Fargo.

"Get against that wall, Fargo."

Blake Griffin stepped into the room, along with the sheriff and the other two men. McCain roused himself, sitting up painfully. He glanced across at the sheriff and then did a double take. Fargo, watching McCain, saw that something had startled McCain about the sheriff. He remembered the trapper saying he'd never met Thomas before, the man that Sitting Elk called the White Friend. Griffin held his derringer before him, his reptilian eyes steady on Fargo.

"You should have told me what was going on in the first place," Fargo said in a friendly voice to Griffin. This was a big gamble, but it was his only chance of escape. "If you'd told me from the beginning why those men were attacking me and McCain up by the lake, we could have been real helpful to you."

"Oh yeah?" Blake Griffin asked suspiciously.

"Yeah," Fargo said. "Until I figured out what your deal was with the gold claims and witnessed that board meeting, I thought you were after me personally. If you or Sheriff Thomas had explained it to me, I could have helped you out."

"I hardly need your help, Mr. Fargo."

"Oh?" Fargo said. "You're about to go attack the Utes in their winter camp."

"So? What of it?"

"So, you need my help in finding the back entrance to the Never Winter Canyon," Fargo lied.

"The only way into that canyon is the turnoff on the trail up to Skull Pass," Griffin protested.

"Nope," Fargo insisted. "There's another way only the Utes know. And it's guarded by only one brave. I bet not even Sheriff Thomas knows about it, and he's a good pal of Sitting Elk's. I found it one day while tracking one of those Utes. You launch a sneak attack on them from that direction and the Utes will never expect it."

Griffin looked at him for a long moment, his eyes narrow. Fargo realized the dwarf was beginning to consider the proposition. He tried to keep the hope off his face.

"I don't give a shit about how many men I lose," Griffin said quietly. None of the men standing outside in the darkness could hear what Griffin was saying. And those were the very men, the innocent prospectors who had come to Martindale hoping to get rich and now had been sucked into a battle with the Utes, who were going to be led into slaughter. All to make it look like the valley was under attack from the Utes, so the senators would vote to nullify the treaty.

"In fact," Griffin added, "the more men I lose, the better it looks back in Washington."

Fargo swore to himself while keeping the smile on his face. Goddamn. He needed an ace up his sleeve right about now. Suddenly he thought of one.

"What about Miss Lily?" Fargo asked. "If that attack goes badly, the Utes will kill her for sure."

"What do you mean?" The voice was the sheriff's, angry and afraid. Fargo had suspected the crooked lawman was sweet on the dark-eyed dove.

"Your old friend Sitting Elk has got Miss Lily. Utes chased us just south of town and she fell off her horse," Fargo lied. "We would have been killed if we'd tried to save her."

"You bastard!" Sheriff Thomas swore, and barreled toward him.

A gunshot split the air, the bullet splintering into the wooden floor. The sheriff halted as Blake Griffin's whispery voice broke the silence.

"Keep control of yourself, Thomas," Griffin said. "There are plenty more ladies around. When this deal goes through, you'll be richer than you've ever dreamed possible. You can buy any woman you want."

A cold glint of suspicion still remained in Griffin's eyes as he moved closer, gazing into Fargo's face. Fargo realized that what he said next would make the difference between whether Griffin shot him here and now or took the chance that he was telling the truth.

"Look," Fargo said, shrugging. "What you do in

this valley is of no interest to me. I only got involved because somebody jumped me. You've heard my reputation. Folks call me the Trailsman. I usually get good money for jobs like this. But in your case, I'm just willing to do it in exchange for my life. And McCain's. It's that simple."

Blake Griffin's stare was like icicles boring through him. Fargo kept his lake-blue eyes steady and his face expressionless. If Griffin had the smallest inkling that Fargo was lying, he'd have him shot.

"He's lying," Griffin said. "There is no back entrance to this Indian camp. And even if there is, so what? If a few Utes escape, there'll just be a few more prospectors killed. The more bloodshed, the quicker our distinguished senators in Washington will vote to deed the entire valley to the law-abiding citizens of Martindale. Lock 'em up in the cell. We'll shoot 'em and then get this attack on the trail tomorrow morning, before the boys cool off."

The sheriff motioned Fargo toward the barred cell. Fargo leaned down to help McCain to his feet. The old trapper's face was gray and blood darkened one side of his shirt.

"I need a doc for my friend," Fargo said.

"What for?" Griffin asked over his shoulder as he left the office. "You're both going to die soon."

The other men stood around, their guns trained on Fargo as he dragged McCain into the cell. The old trapper was in pain, just barely holding onto his consciousness.

"At least you could get me some morphine. Or

whiskey," Fargo pleaded as Sheriff Thomas locked the door behind them. The sheriff nodded toward one of the men, who left and returned shortly with a bottle of red-eye. Then Thomas left, leaving one of the men to stand guard.

It was a long, cold night. Fargo had laid the old trapper out on the bare rope bed and covered him with the thin blanket. McCain was shivering, his eyes distant. Fargo tried to make the man comfortable, and even tore up his shirt to fashion a bandage for his stomach wound, to slow the bleeding, but McCain was done for and they both knew it. He went in and out of his mind, ranting about beaver skins and deer hunting and some woman named Cassie he'd loved back in Illinois when he was a boy.

Toward morning, Fargo looked up to see the sheriff standing outside the bars, watching as Fargo held the liquor to the trapper's mouth. McCain took a swig and sputtered. "Nothing's going to help me now," he muttered. Fargo took off his jacket, balled it up, and propped up the old man's head. McCain's eyes focused on the sheriff. "I thought . . . you were the Utes' good friend."

Sheriff Thomas shifted uneasily. "One time, the chief thought I saved him from a bear," Thomas said curtly. "Sitting Elk has called me White Friend ever since." The sheriff chuckled to himself. "Stupid redskin," he added.

Fargo glanced at the trapper and saw on his face the same thoughts he was having. He remembered the story McCain had told in the cabin, about seeing the white man sneaking up on Sitting Elk and about to kill him and then being surprised by the bear. Obviously that had been the sheriff, and he had talked his way out of it. Made the chief and the whole tribe think he'd just saved the chief's life.

"I saw you," McCain said, his broken words spoken with great effort. "I was up in the bushes. I knew you were about to kill that Indian. And I almost shot you myself." McCain looked up at the ceiling. "If only I had," he muttered to himself. "If only I had."

As Fargo watched, the light left his eyes. McCain was dead. Fargo felt the black rage swell inside him. Rage at this goddamn town of rich crooks, at the sheriff's duplicity toward Sitting Elk, at the death of the innocent McCain. The anger was like an earthquake that began as a rumble deep inside him and then intensified, threatening to split him apart.

"He dead?" the sheriff asked.

Fargo glanced up to see the sheriff peering between the bars of the cell. With a hoarse cry, Fargo leaped like a cougar straight toward the surprised sheriff, gripping the neck of the bottle of red-eye in one fist. Sheriff Thomas backed away, but not fast enough. As Fargo smashed against the bars of the cell, he reached out with his free hand and grabbed hold of the sheriff's collar, jerking him forward. With the other hand, he smashed the bottle against the bars. The red-eye spattered everywhere and Fargo held the crown of broken glass before him, intending to butcher the sheriff, to slice him apart.

But the sheriff slumped to the floor, the impact of the iron bars having stunned him. He groaned, half conscious, and fumbled for his gun, his eyelids fluttering. The rage died in Fargo and the cold, clear-eyed desire for revenge took hold. Goddamn, he'd make them pay for all of this, he swore.

Moving quickly, he pulled the heavy body of the sheriff nearer, slid the gun from his holster, and hit him on the skull. The ring of keys had fallen out of the sheriff's pocket and lay just out of reach. Fargo stretched his arm through the bars, holding the pistol, and was just able to snag the ring with the long barrel. In a moment, the keys were in his hand and he let himself out of the cell. He gagged the sheriff and dragged him behind the bars. With a last glance toward McCain's inert body on the cot, Fargo locked the cell door, gathered up his Colt, and moved toward the broken door of the sheriff's office. He spotted a big, plaid wool coat and a fur hat on a peg. He quickly donned them. In the dark, wearing other clothes, nobody would be likely to recognize him.

Through the window, Fargo glimpsed the sky. A gray light lit the east and the sky was deep in clouds. Fargo heard the sound of shouting and of men preparing for battle. He eased the splintered door open slowly and looked out. At the far end of the block men were saddling horses, and several mountain wagons stood waiting. They looked like the same wagons that had come into town with the winter supplies for the Indians, except that instead of being filled with crates and kegs, the wagons stood empty. Fargo slid along the side of the building, staying in its shadow. As he watched, Burly Joe directed some of the men to practice hunching down inside the wagons.

So that was their plan, thought Fargo. They were going to roll the wagons into the middle of the Ute camp, pretending they were bringing the winter supplies. And then they would come out, guns blazing, to catch the Utes completely by surprise.

If he could just warn the Utes, they might have a fighting chance, Fargo realized. If some Utes came forward unarmed while others, guns trained on the wagons, hid among the trees, the Indians could easily win. But his big problem now was to get out of town. Fargo raised the collar of the plaid jacket and walked nonchalantly along the boardwalk, heading toward the crowd.

Fargo melted easily into the group of men who were piling rifles into the wagons and getting the horses hitched to the wagons. One horse, a strong palomino, balked at the traces.

"She's too spirited," one man said. He turned toward Fargo and handed him the reins. "Get this one back to the stables." He called out for some one to bring over another horse. Fargo nodded, smiling to himself, and moved off down the street. Once out of sight, he mounted the horse and rode slowly down the road that led out of town. He had to pass by the Martindale Hotel. As the massive three-story building with the towering cupola came into sight, he saw in front a string of horses, saddled and waiting, and men scurrying about. In the center, loaded with large saddlebags, Fargo spotted his black-and-white Ovaro.

He pulled up on the palomino then walked it into an alley, where he turned about and sat watching. In a moment, the small figure of Blake Griffin emerged from the front of the hotel, along with about a dozen other men. In a moment, Fargo recognized the board members of the Gold Club. The men were bundled up to their teeth in fur coats and hats and fine leather boots. Probably had their gold watch fobs on underneath, too, he thought.

Griffin was speaking to the men, but Fargo was too far away to make out the words. What the hell was going on? Then he remembered about the payment that was going to Washington. He realized that the Gold Club members were all making a trip to the capital to deliver the two hundred and fifty thousand dollars of bribes to be paid to Griffin's brother, Senator Joshua Griffin. And his own horse, the magnificent Ovaro, was carrying the money. Whoever had stolen his pinto had probably been damn frustrated. The trusty horse didn't let anyone on its back but Fargo. That explained why it was now loaded with the cash.

The cold wind was blowing at his back, and as he watched, Fargo saw the Ovaro raise its head and nicker, then turn to look toward him. The pinto had picked up his scent. Fargo realized that there was nothing he could do to rescue the horse now. Not yet.

He rode the palomino down the short alley and was soon out of town. Nobody stopped him or gave chase, so obviously they hadn't discovered the sheriff yet.

The palomino was surefooted and lively, Fargo thought appreciatively as he turned it up the left fork of the road that led out of Martindale. It was a good ten miles to the top of Skull Pass, and halfway along the narrow trail was the turnoff to the Never Winter Canyon, where the Utes stayed during the cold months.

As his horse scrambled up the steep trail, Fargo thought of the difficulty the men would have bringing the mountain wagons up toward the cut-off. The damn wagons had been brought all the way over the pass in the first place, Fargo thought. And it was just typical of the U.S. government and the Indian Bureau that, rather than being delivered directly to the winter camp, they had been taken all the way to town so the Indian agent could sign for them. And steal from them, Fargo thought bitterly. Typical bureaucracy, he thought. Do things the hardest way possible.

The light was growing in the east. It would be a bad day, he saw, bitterly cold with more snow on the way. The clouds were heavy with it. The tall, dark pines around him were shrouded with white, and as he ascended the trail, winding back and forth up the narrow switchbacks, the snow grew deeper. There were dimpled tracks. Several horses had come this way the day before. Fargo knew they were the tracks of Sitting Elk and his men. Fargo tried to imagine how Waiting Cloud and Lily were getting along by now.

The cutoff to the Ute winter camp was just ahead. Fargo took the turn and the palomino plunged down the slope, descending into the valley between the pines. The country was still and quiet, the only sound the whistle of the wind in the top of the trees and the chatter of a few early-rising jays.

Fargo had gone only a half a mile up the canyon when he heard the metallic click of a rifle from the left side of him. He pulled up on the horse as a Ute brave stepped out from behind a tree. "I'm looking for Sitting Elk," Fargo said. He recognized one of the braves who had come to the cabin, so he quickly removed his fur hat.

The brave peered at him. "You are Dark of Night." He waved him on.

Fargo's horse plunged through the deep snow for another mile as the yellow canyon walls rose up around him. Soon the walls fell away and he came to an almost perfectly round bowl. Sunlight poured in and the low canyon walls seemed to reflect what light came from the wide sky above, while the tall, encircling peaks shielded the place from the bitter winds. This was Never Winter Canyon.

The Utes' wickiups and tipis stood in the center. Smoke from the cooking fires rose against the sky. A few dark-green stands of pines dotted the white-blanketed expanse. Most of the tribe seemed to be huddled in their shelters and only a few women could be seen, toting wood or bending over orange fires. A brave approached and halted a few feet from Fargo, who asked to see Sitting Elk.

Fargo was led to a large buffalo-skin tipi. The brave motioned him inside. A small fire crackled in the center of the round tent, and thick buffalo skins and woven rugs covered the ground. Sitting Elk sat before the fire as if he had been waiting for Fargo. That was one thing about Indians, Fargo thought. They never seemed to be taken by surprise.

Waiting Cloud sat nearby, stitching two skins together. Her face brightened when she saw Fargo. Next to her sat Lily, her dark hair tangled and her face woebegone.

"It's about time you came to get me," Lily snapped at Fargo. "Living in this pigsty is—"

"I'm not here for you," Fargo snapped back at her. "So shut up."

Lily fell silent. Waiting Cloud handed her a couple of skins, directing her to sew them. Lily plunged the needle into one and stuck herself, sucked on her finger, and shot hateful looks at Fargo.

Fargo sat down cross-legged and Sitting Elk began to fill the pipe. "There is trouble in the white camp," the old chief remarked, passing the lit pipe to Fargo.

Fargo was glad they were getting down to business right away. There wasn't much time. "Big trouble," he replied. "The men are planning an attack on this camp. They're bringing the mountain wagons, but instead of food inside, there are men

145

with guns. You and your people will be slaughtered."

The chief showed no surprise as he puffed the pipe. "It is like my dream," he said. "Now the white man even come to this small canyon, the small tipi of the Utes."

"And Sheriff Thomas is involved," Fargo said. "I'm sorry to tell you he's the one who's been stealing your supplies. He's not your friend." Fargo related the story that McCain had told him.

"I remember well," the chief said. "Yes, at first I thought when I turned around 'this white man means to shoot me.' But there was the bear, shot dead. I liked this man's face. And I believed him."

"So did I," said Fargo. "But in addition to trying to starve you out, and attacking, they're going to get your treaty revoked."

The chief looked puzzled. "What means this word? *Revoked*?"

"Uh, nullified. Void," Fargo said. The chief still looked confused, so Fargo tried again. "To make it like the treaty never existed. To make the treaty go away."

"White men," the chief said sadly, shaking his head. "They believe they can make things go away and they even have a word for it. Revoked. Revoked." Sitting Elk looked up at Fargo and smiled suddenly. "I would like to *revoked* the white man coming to this valley," he said.

"I'll bet you would," Fargo said. "But meanwhile, we've got to make some plans. Those wagons will

be here soon and we need to get your men into position so they'll be ready. There's no time to waste."

It was mid-morning and snow was falling hard
when word came by runner that the mountain
wagons had been sighted heading up the trail.
Fargo and Sitting Elk stood by the tipis waiting.
The wagons would arrive in a half hour. Fargo
glanced around at the tufts of dark trees which
loomed against the swirling snow. Each bristled
with Utes hidden among the trunks, fully armed
and ready to fire into the wagons. The women and
children had been hidden beneath a rock overhang
at the back of the canyon. A few braves dressed as
women tended the fires, so as not to arouse suspicion.

In the snowstorm, it was impossible to see far.
That might be to their advantage, Fargo thought.
There was no way the Martindale men would spot
the Utes hidden in the trees. But he hoped to
make the men see reason before the firing started.
If there was an all-out battle, many of the men
killed would be the innocent prospectors who were
being manipulated by the sheriff and Griffin. He
hoped he could find a way to avert slaughter on
both sides.

Fargo slipped off into the chief's tipi when word
came that the mountain wagons had turned onto
the cutoff. Waiting Cloud and Lily sat there, in
nervous anticipation. Fargo had insisted on keeping
Lily close by in case she could be used to persuade
the sheriff to give it up. And Waiting Cloud had re-

fused to go with the other women. He hastily changed clothes, pulling on Indian buckskins and throwing a buffalo robe around his shoulders.

Finally, Fargo heard the creak of wagons as they entered the canyon bowl. He left the tent and walked toward Sitting Elk, standing slightly behind him in the midst of some other braves, all of whom had rifles held beneath the heavy buffalo and deer-skin robes they wore against the cold. The chief had insisted on doing the talking.

Sheriff Thomas rode way behind the wagons, along with Burly Joe. Another man, red-bearded, a prospector by the look of him, led. Even from a distance, Fargo could see the bruise darkening the sheriff's face and left eye where he'd banged into the cell bars. Fargo smiled to himself.

The sheriff was nervous, jumpy. He kept looking around to one side and then to the other. He was scared, Fargo thought, probably wondering if Fargo had escaped and tipped off the Utes about the attack. Suddenly Fargo was nervous too. It was possible the sheriff was smarter than he'd anticipated. After all, the sheriff had stuck this red-bearded man up front like a sacrificial lamb, the first to be killed when the shooting started. The wagons stopped and the red-bearded man raised one hand.

"How," he said, grunting. The man was shaking and had obviously never spoken to an Indian in his life, Fargo thought. Sitting Elk turned toward his braves and rolled his eyes. Without looking at the red-bearded man again, he walked slowly around him, passing by the mountain wagons and heading

148

toward where the sheriff waited, well behind the wagons. The chief was damned brave, Fargo thought. At any moment, a hundred men could pop out of those wagons and he'd be dead. And the chief knew it. But still he walked toward the sheriff, the man he had called White Friend, the man who had betrayed him.

Several of the braves broke off from the waiting group and followed their chief. Fargo went with them, keeping them between himself and the sheriff so he wouldn't be recognized.

"You have brought me food, White Friend?" the chief said to Sheriff Thomas.

"I always stick by my friends," the sheriff said grandly, gesturing toward the wagons. "Inside you'll find plenty to keep you going the whole winter. Just call your people out and they can start unloading. Then we'll take the wagons back to town."

So that was it, Fargo thought. The whole village assembled and the cover taken off the wagons and a hundred men suddenly standing up and shooting.

"But first, I hear you've got a white woman here," the sheriff said, his eyes flitting over the tipis. "Now, Chief, you know I can't give you this food if you're holding a white woman."

Sitting Elk nodded. "I did not know she belonged to you," he said. He sent one of the braves to fetch Lily, and another toward the wagons.

"Now hold on a moment," the sheriff said, suddenly looking frightened as the brave approached the wagon. The drivers of the wagons scrambled down off their seats and headed toward the sheriff.

A gust of wind blew the snow around them. The sheriff glanced behind him. "You get your people out here to unload those wagons first." His voice sounded tense, scared.

"We will look inside," said the chief impassively. Fargo felt the braves standing around him shifting slightly as they pulled their rifles up inside their robes. They were damned brave, these Utes, he thought with admiration. They were willing to stand there, with no protection but their own rifles and their own wits, ready to face the hundred guns that would explode out of those wagons any second now. And Sitting Elk betrayed absolutely no fear.

"Thomas!" Lily called out. Waiting Cloud chased her across the snowy expanse as Lily ran toward the sheriff. "They know everything!" Lily screamed. "Fargo is here!" The Indian woman took a flying leap and tackled Lily, throwing her to the ground.

Just then, the brave threw back the canvas cover from the wagon. Nothing happened. No guns, no men. The wagons were empty.

Fargo glanced up at the sheriff, whose face was pale, his eyes shifting nervously. He pulled his pistol and fired over his head twice, obviously a signal to attack. He and Burly Joe started to pull their horses about just as Fargo saw movement among the trees at the entrance to the canyon.

In a flash, Fargo realized what had happened. The sheriff had been wilier than he'd suspected. Thomas had worried that Fargo might tip off the Utes and he'd sent the wagons in empty. The men had followed, unseen by the scouts in the blinding snow. They must have overpowered the guards at the entrance to the canyon. And now they were attacking, pouring in from the trees, their horses streaking out of the dark trunks. The Utes hidden in the stands of pines surrounding the village held their fire, waiting until the Martindale men were clear of cover. The braves standing around Fargo brought their rifles up and threw themselves onto the snowy ground, aiming toward where the attackers would break out of the trees at any moment.

Sitting Elk, standing near the sheriff, reached up and grabbed the saddle horn just as the sheriff brought his horse around. Thomas's horse galloped toward the trees, dragging the chief with him as the sheriff clubbed at him. Fargo leaped up as Burly Joe's horse reared and came down heavily. Fargo pulled Burly Joe down off the horse and smashed his fist into the wide jaw. Bone crunched beneath his knuckles. Joe staggered backward and then sank to his knees and fell forward. Fargo jumped onto Joe's horse and tore off after Sheriff Thomas and the chief, straight into the line of Martindale men advancing among the trees. Burly Joe's horse was fast and the sheriff's mount was hampered by the extra weight of two men. Just then, Fargo saw Sitting Elk bring his legs up and thrust them between the two front legs of the running horse.

The horse screamed and went down heavily. Fargo's horse overtook them, and he jumped down and threw himself onto the ground just as the sheriff's horse rolled to one side. The chief lay in the snow facing Sheriff Thomas, one wiry hand around the sheriff's throat and another, with a knife, poised above his neck. The sheriff's horse had rolled on top of him and it was clear he had only a few moments to live. A thin stream of bright-red blood ran out of the corner of Sheriff Thomas's mouth. His eyes were wide and scared as he looked at the knife in Sitting Elk's hand.

The line of men had just appeared among the trees, galloping on horseback. In a moment, they'd be right on top of them. "Call off the attack," Fargo shouted at the sheriff.

The sheriff's eyes, pain-dimmed, looked at Fargo and recognized him.

"There are a hundred Utes hiding in the trees. The game's up."

The sheriff fumbled for his gun but Fargo kicked away his hand. "How many shots?" Fargo asked, pulling up his rifle.

"Five fast ones," the sheriff whispered. Fargo raised his rifle and shot into the air, five times, fast.

The line of attacking men slowed, then wavered and stopped. The men drew together, uncertain of what to do next. They held their rifles, still ready.

Fargo threw off the buffalo robe and struggled out of the deerskin shirt to show the plaid shirt he wore underneath. He walked out toward the line of men. "I'm Skye Fargo!" he shouted. "Three of you men come here!"

The men looked at one another, puzzled, and three of them hesitantly rode forward. Fargo instructed them to dismount and then led them over to where the sheriff lay dying.

"Why were you attacking the Utes?" Fargo shot at the sheriff. Thomas didn't respond at first, but then his eyes cleared and he focused on Fargo.

"Grab their land. Griffin's idea," he muttered.

"Is there any gold in this valley?" Fargo asked.

"No, no," Thomas answered. "We salt the claims. Griffin makes money on the rent. We all make money."

"And how do you make your money?" Fargo asked.

The blood was now pouring from the sheriff's mouth and he spoke with great difficulty. "Sell the supplies. Indian supplies."

Just then Lily came running, followed by Waiting Cloud. "Thomas!" she screamed, seeing the blood on the snow.

"I did it . . . for you, Lily," the sheriff said, his words thick and almost incomprehensible. His eyes opened wide and then his head sagged to one side. Lily threw herself down on top of him.

The three men Fargo had called over looked at each other in astonishment. "You mean this whole thing is a scam?" one of them asked.

"If you want proof, go look in the back room of the land-claim office," Fargo said. "There never were any gold strikes here. Just a bunch of greedy landowners."

"Salting the claims," another said. "Wait until word of this gets around."

"Thanks for getting to the truth," one of the men

said, shaking Fargo's hand. The three of them walked back toward the waiting crowd and Fargo could see the whole group of them huddling. By afternoon every prospector in the valley would know the story, and by tomorrow the valley would be almost deserted.

Fargo turned toward the chief.

"Horse broke my legs," Sitting Elk said, as if in mild surprise. His legs lay on the snow in two broken angles. Two braves came and carried the old chief toward the tipis.

Waiting Cloud looked expectantly at Fargo. "Come and rest," she said.

"There's still a piece of unfinished business," Fargo said, shaking his head. He strode toward the group of prospectors waiting on horseback. He'd seen them stirred up and ready for battle. And now he was about to stir them up again. Only this time against Blake Griffin.

Fargo rode the palomino, followed by twenty of the men from Martindale. They picked their way steadily up the trail against the blowing snow. They left behind the tall pines as they ascended. At this high altitude, the dwarf pines, low to the ground and almost buried in the snow, had been twisted by the relentless wind. The steep slopes, deep with unbroken white, loomed high above them, disappearing into the whiteness above. They had just rounded a curve when Fargo spotted, through the storm, the prominent rock wall with the two deep caves in its face that gave the trail its name—Skull Pass.

And he also spotted a dozen horses, dark shadows in the blowing storm, trekking up the trail ahead of them toward the top of the pass. His keen eyes found the dim shape of his black-and-white Ovaro in the center of the line, loaded with the money to pay off the senators in Washington. He also picked out the short man riding at the head of the line. He felt the red rage well in him at the sight of Blake Griffin. He couldn't wait to get his hands around the little creep's neck.

Fargo gave his horse a swift kick and the palomino pushed forward through the thick snow, its heavy breath smoking in the thin, bitter air. Just then, one of the men in line turned about and spotted them. In a moment, Fargo saw, the line of a dozen men had spurred their horses forward, straining to escape. The palomino struggled to move faster. Fargo spurred the horse again and the gap between them closed.

He was just about to draw his Colt when Griffin turned around in his saddle. Without a pause, he aimed straight at Fargo and fired. Fargo felt the tearing pain of the shot through his right arm. He grabbed his arm and swore. Goddamn, his shooting arm. The echo of the gunshot seemed swallowed by the thick air, filled with falling snow. In the instant that followed, Fargo heard another sound. A sound he'd heard only once before and never forgotten. A whispering, shimmering sound, as if ocean waves were sliding up a beach far away. It was a mysterious sound, that not many men had heard and lived to remember, but Fargo knew what it meant. It was the sound of tons of snow slithering down a mountainside, touched off by the noise of Griffin's gun.

The men behind him drew up their rifles, but before they could fire, Fargo yelled, "Avalanche! Go back!"

Pandemonium broke out as the men tried to turn their horses about on the narrow trail. Fargo peered into the blowing snow at the snaking line of horses ahead on the trail. The shimmering noise increased until it sounded like waves breaking. The line of horses came to a halt as Griffin stopped and looked upward in confusion. They were all doomed. Fargo puckered his lips and whistled.

The pinto in the center of the line reacted immediately. It reared and came about, plunging a few feet off to one side before heading straight for them. Fargo heard Blake Griffin call out, and the sound of another shot, before the clouds of snow obliterated his vision.

The roar of the sliding snow increased and he heard one of the men yell. The blizzard swirled about and Fargo could see nothing as the avalanche poured down the side of the mountain, throwing up an impenetrable fog of snow. Behind him, the men of Martindale had retreated down the trail, but Fargo waited in the swirling white, feeling the snow beat about him and hoping he was clear of the fall line.

The shouts and screams and gunfire ahead of

him increased and then ceased as he heard only the rumble of the avalanche. Suddenly Fargo saw a dark flash and the Ovaro struggled out of a snow drift, nickering. Fargo jumped off the palomino and the pinto came toward him out of the whiteness, whinnying and stamping.

Fargo looked past the horse into the blinding white. Blake Griffin and the dozen men of the Gold Club were dead. Buried alive beneath tons of snow and ice. It served them right. And Martindale was free of them at last. Fargo turned away and led the two horses down the trail to where the other men waited, then loaded the saddlebags onto the palomino and mounted the Ovaro. The line of men started down the trail.

When he got back to town, Fargo decided, they'd divide up the money. The prospectors could get some back. And the Utes would get money for the supplies they never received. He'd get his arm tended by the doctor. And when all that was done, he thought, he had one more piece of unfinished business.

He needed to thank a certain dark woman in an ivory dress, he thought with a smile. And he intended to thank her properly.

LOOKING FORWARD!
The following is the opening
section from the next novel in the exciting
Trailsman series from Signet:

THE TRAILSMAN #155
OKLAHOMA ORDEAL

1860, the Oklahoma/Texas border country,
where men rode at their own risk,
and women were fair game . . .

At first Skye Fargo thought the keening sound he
heard was the wind. A storm loomed on the western horizon, and already the breeze had picked up
to the point where it imitated a banshee. But when
the mournful wail was repeated, he knew instantly
the sound came from a human throat.

Reining up, the big man rose in the stirrups of
his pinto stallion and surveyed the rolling prairie
on either side of the rutted trail he followed. Other
than the rippling of the grass there was no hint of
movement, no trace of another human being.

Fargo pushed his white hat back on his head and
idly scratched his chin. He was too seasoned a

plainsman for his ears to be playing tricks on him. There had to be someone out there, someone in trouble. And judging by the scream, that someone was a woman.

Clucking the Ovaro forward, Fargo slowly rode to the southwest, loosening his Colt in its holster as a sensible precaution. A lone rider never knew when trouble might rear its unwanted head, either from hostile Indians, savage beasts, or outlaws whose savagery made the beasts seem tame by comparison.

Suddenly the cry was repeated a third time. Fargo pinpointed the direction, due north, and lightly applied his spurs to the stallion's flanks. He shucked the pistol, holding it close to his thigh.

The prairie could be deceptive. A man might think it went on forever, flat and unchanged mile after mile, when in truth, a gully or ravine or dry wash might be a stone's throw away. This time it was the latter, sixty yards from the trail.

Fargo heard muffled voices and slowed to a walk so he wouldn't advertise his presence. His sharp eyes saw where a wagon had crushed the grass within the past hour or so as it rolled to the gently sloping rim of the wash, then down over. Halting, he slid off and padded closer to investigate.

A wagon of the sort favored by drummers rested at the bottom, its team standing at rest. Nearby were six people. Three hard cases ringed an older man in a faded black suit and black derby who was flat on his back with blood trickling from the corner of his mouth. A pair of young women were to one side, both pretty fillies blessed by nature with the sort of looks that made Fargo's blood race and his mouth go dry.

As Fargo watched, a blond woman launched herself at a string bean of a man, screeching, "You leave him alone, damn you!"

Quick as a panther the man whirled, catching hold of both her wrists before she could pummel him. "Calm down, missy," he snapped. "This old geezer has this comin' and he's going to take his licks whether you like it or not."

"You have no call to be doing this to our pa!" declared the other woman, a brunette whose curly locks cascaded to the small of her slender back.

"I reckon we do," said another man, nudging her father with the toe of his boot. "This bastard should have gotten his due a long time ago."

"We'll report you to the law!" countered the brunette.

Two of the men chuckled and the string bean shoved the blond from him. "Go right ahead, ma'am," he said. "I'm sure any lawdog in the territory would be mighty interested in your doings."

The third hombre, a grizzled hard case whose steely eyes glittered with spite, bent down to roughly haul the older man erect. "Enough jawing," he barked. "It's time we got down to business. I got me a hankering to reach Guthrie by nightfall."

Without warning he slammed a fist into the old man's gut, doubling him over.

"Damn you!" cried the brunette, springing to her father's defense. She was seized by the second man.

The blond promptly tried once more to intervene and was again grabbed by the skinny one, who commented, "Do what we came for, Jeb. These ladies won't be botherin' you none."

Fargo saw Jeb punch the old man in the stomach a second time. When the father sank to his knees, sputtering, Fargo stood, leveled the Colt, and cocked the hammer. The metallic click caused the three hard cases to glance up sharply.

"Who the hell are you?" String Bean blurted.

"What do you want?" demanded Jeb.

Fargo wagged his pistol at three horses ground-hitched a score of feet down the wash. "I want you to mount up and head out."

"This ain't none of your affair," String Bean said.

"That's right," chimed in Jeb. "We won't take it kindly if you stick your nose in where it don't belong."

"I don't care how you take it," Fargo said, advancing carefully down the incline. "Just so you leave before my trigger finger twitches."

String Bean released the blond. "Are you with this bunch?" he asked angrily. "If so, I'm warnin' you here and now that you're askin' for a heap of grief."

The third man nodded as he pushed the brunette. "That's the gospel truth, mister. We look out after our own. There'll be hell to pay for what's been done."

"There'll be hell to pay if you don't fork leather," Fargo warned, tiring of their empty threats.

Scowling, the trio backed toward their mounts. Jeb dragged his heels, his right hand poised above his six-shooter, fingers clawed, twitching eagerly.

"I'd think twice if I was you," Fargo stated. To emphasize his point he slanted the Colt and stroked the trigger.

Jeb uttered a yelp, clutching his right ear. When he lowered his hand there was blood on his fingers. "You son of a bitch!" he roared. "You shot my ear off!"

"I only nicked it," Fargo said. "And if you're not out of here in one minute I'll aim a couple of inches to the left."

Grumbling and glaring, the three climbed on their horses. At the top of the wash they each looked back, hatred lining their features—especially Jeb's. String Bean voiced a whoop and all three galloped off in a cloud of dust.

Skye Fargo began reloading his six-gun in case they returned. The drum of hoofbeats gradually receded, fading in due course to silence. Only then did the women and the old man stir to life.

"Thank heaven you came to our rescue, sir!" the

blond said. "There's no telling what those ruffians would have done to our poor pa."

"We can never thank you enough," added the brunette.

"I'm sure you could if you tried," Fargo responded, grinning and meeting her frank gaze with a suggestive look.

Their father coughed and touched his split lip. "I dare say this sort of thing is all too common on the frontier. A man in my profession is always treated shabbily by the rougher element." Extending his arm, he said, "But enough about those scalawags. Where are my manners? I'm Phinneas T. Boggs, at your service, my good man. And these lovelies are my daughters, Liberty—," he gestured at the blond, "—and Belle." He nodded at the brunette.

"You're pulling my leg," Fargo said.

"Never, sir," Phinneas replied. "Ask anyone. A lie has never passed these lips." He removed his derby and wiped a sleeve across his perspiring brow. "My wife, bless her departed soul, was from Philadelphia. Patriotic to the core, she was." Phinneas smirked. "Actually, I should count my blessing she didn't name our girls Betsy and Ross."

The spent cartridge replaced, Fargo twirled the Colt into his holster.

Liberty whistled. "You're right handy with that shooting iron, aren't you?"

"I've had some practice," Fargo allowed. He glanced at the wagon and for the first time noticed the words painted on the wooden side. "PHINNEAS BOGGS," he read aloud. "MIRACLE CURES FOR EVERY AILMENT."

"No idle boast," Phinneas said proudly. "I've plied my trade for nigh thirty years now. There isn't a sickness I haven't treated, an injury I haven't fixed."

"You're a patent medicine man," Fargo said, abruptly suspicious. Patent medicine men were notorious throughout the West as the biggest liars and cheats in all creation. They traveled from town to town offering to cure everything under the sun, but many of their so-called medicines turned out to be worthless concoctions that often did their patients more harm than good. He stared in the direction taken by the hard cases, wondering.

The older man squared his shoulders. "That I am," he declared. "And I can tell by your face what you're thinking. But you misjudge me, sir. There are thousands of grateful people from here to the Mississippi who will testify to my ability and integrity."

"What about those men?" Fargo asked. "Did you sell them some of your medicine?"

"As God is my witness, no," Phinneas said gravely.

"All my pa did was stand up to them when they tried to take advantage of Liberty and me," Belle said.

"That's right," her sister agreed. "They wanted to

buy us drinks back in Guthrie and when we refused they took it badly. So the vermin followed us all this way. Not ten minutes ago they forced Pa to drive off the trail so no one would interfere while they did as they pleased. Only you saved us," Liberty breathed, brazenly taking hold of Fargo's arm and giving it a gentle squeeze. She studied his whipcord frame, the pink tip of her tongue poking between her cherry lips.

"You wouldn't happen to be on your way to Rawbone, would you?" Phinneas inquired.

Fargo was on his way to Texas, where he had an appointment to keep with a man who wanted to hire him to track down a band of cutthroats responsible for murdering the man's family. Rawbone lay on his route, not twenty miles further. "I'll be passing through," he revealed.

"Excellent!" Phinneas said. "In that case, perhaps you'd consent to ride with us the rest of the way? It would put my mind at ease knowing my daughters had such a capable protector."

Liberty squealed in delight and squeezed Fargo harder. "Oh, please do! We haven't had anyone else to talk to for three days."

"You won't regret it," Belle added.

The promise in her tone was unmistakable. Fargo admired the tantalizing swell of her hips and how nicely the brunette filled out her blouse. His manhood twitched, reminding him of the week and a half he'd just spent in the saddle, a week and a half without female companionship. "I'd be happy to ride with you," he said.

"How wonderful!" Liberty exclaimed, impulsively pecking Fargo on the cheek. At a look from her father she let go of the big man's arm and stepped back, bowing her head in apparent embarrassment at her behavior.

"You'll have to excuse my girls," Phinneas said. "Sometimes they're too darn friendly for their own good."

"I don't mind," Fargo said, thinking that they couldn't possibly reach Rawbone before the next afternoon, which meant he'd be spending all night in the company of the two lovelies. There were worse fates.

"Fine," the father said. "Give me a few minutes to get my wagon back on the ground and we'll be on our way."

Nodding, Fargo headed up the slope toward the Ovaro. His head cleared the rim, then his shoulders. He mentally pictured both sisters buck naked with him lying between them, and smirked. Distracted by his lust, he didn't notice the distant glint of sunlight off metal until it was almost too late. He threw himself down as a lead hornet buzzed by. A split second later the crack of a rifle shot rippled across the grassland.

"Damn!" Phinneas cried. "They're still after us!"

Fargo had the Colt out. Removing his hat, he raised high enough to take a hasty peek. He couldn't see the shooter but he knew the man was about sixty yards out, to the west. One of the men, at least, had doubled back. If all three had, he was trapped.

"How dare they!" Liberty said. Dainty fists clenched, she stormed up the slope. "I've had my fill of these jackasses!"

Before the foolish young woman could expose herself, Fargo grabbed a shapely ankle and pulled, upending her on her backside next to him. She let out an indignant squawk, then slapped at his hand.

"What do you think you're doing?"

"Saving your hide," Fargo said.

"They wouldn't shoot a woman," Liberty protested, trying to jerk her leg free.

"They'll put a bullet into anything that moves," Fargo said. Releasing her, he picked up a hefty rock, rolled onto his side, and hurled the rock skyward. Immediately a pair of rifles blasted. The rock shattered, sharp fragments raining down on Fargo and the woman, causing her to flinch. He stared at her and she turned beet-red.

"Sorry, mister. My anger got the better of me."

Phinneas, bent low, joined them. "What can we do? We're pinned down, completely at their mercy."

"I say we fight," Belle declared, moving toward the rear of the wagon. "We've let them push us around long enough." She yanked open a small door and disappeared inside.

Inching upward, Fargo checked on his pinto. The loyal Ovaro was a dozen feet off, exactly where he had left it, patiently awaiting his return. He had to get the animal under cover, and quickly. Inserting two fingers into his mouth, he whistled softly twice. The stallion lifted his head, ears pricked, and swiftly advanced.

Fargo took a calculated gamble to distract the three men from the pinto. Rising on his knees, he fired three times, fanning the pistol. He shifted after each shot, sending a slug to the west, south, and north. There were no targets visible, but that didn't matter. He only wanted to draw their attention and he succeeded admirably.

A ragged volley blistered the rim, slugs punching into the dirt from several directions at once. Fargo ducked down, a reaction the three men would be expecting. But then he did the unexpected; he vaulted from concealment, bounded to the Ovaro, seized the reins, and spun, intending to reach safety before the trio recovered from their surprise and cut loose. In this he failed, for as he turned he spied String Bean to the north, already upright and taking deliberate aim with a Henry. The range was too great for a revolver. For an instant Fargo stared death in the face, the short hairs at the nape of his neck prickling.

A new element was added when another gun thundered before String Bean could fire. Belle had popped up, a rifle tucked to her shoulder. Her shot drove String Bean to ground, buying Fargo the precious seconds needed for him to scoot into the wash. He barely made it when the hard cases peppered the rim.

Belle had flattened and was feeding another cartridge into her rifle. She winked at Fargo and said, "I think I winged him. I would have done better but I rushed on your account."

"I'm grateful," Fargo said. From his saddle scabbard he took his Sharps. Making certain it was loaded, he glided over to her. "Where did you learn to shoot like that?"

"I was a regular tomboy when I was younger," Belle explained rather sheepishly. "At an age when most other girls were playing with dolls or helping their mothers around the house, I was off hunting and fishing. Now Pa counts on me to supply game for the table whenever we're on the go."

Fargo moved past her to the top. Using his thumb he cocked the Sharps, then pulled the rear trigger to set the front trigger for the slightest of pressure. The three hard cases were nowhere to be seen, but he doubted they had gone—not when they wanted to get their hands on the sisters badly enough to kill anyone who stood in their way.

Going prone, Fargo wedged the heavy rifle to his shoulder. He held the barrel low to the ground to reduce the gleam of sunshine off the metal surface. Elbows firmly propped, he scanned the wash, which was cast in shadow by oncoming storm clouds. The wind had intensified even more, bringing with it the dank scent of moisture.

"This is all we need!" Phinneas remarked, regarding the overcast western sky with annoyance.

Fargo shifted to inform Boggs that the rain might work in their favor. He happened to spy a lanky figure fifty yards out, darting from north to east. Instantly he swiveled, swinging the Sharps as he turned. A hasty bead had to suffice, and then he stroked the trigger.

Arms flapping, the figure twisted and flew backwards to vanish in high weeds.

"Did you get one?" Belle asked hopefully.

"Maybe," Fargo said, reloading.

Gunfire erupted from two directions, a senseless fusillade that spewed geysers of dirt from the rim.

"They're mad as wet hens," Belle said gleefully. "You must have made wolf meat of one of the buzzards."

Gradually the shooting died off and for several minutes all was quiet, until the rumble of far-off thunder heralded strong gusts of wind and a light spattering of raindrops.

Phinneas and Liberty scooted over, the father saying anxiously, "What do you suggest we do? They can slip in here under cover of the storm and pick us off one by one."

"That works both ways," Fargo said, indicating the wagon. "I want you to get set to move on out like a bat out of hell when I give you the word."

"Is that wise? My wagon is too heavy to take this slope very fast," Phinneas hedged. "We'll be like clay targets in a shooting gallery."

"Not if I keep them busy," Fargo stated in a tone that made it clear he was in no mood for an argument.

"But if something should happen to my dear daughters—," Phinneas said, leaving the thought unfinished.

"You were the one who asked for my help, remember?" Fargo reminded him. "Either we do this my way or you can fend for yourselves."

Reluctantly the older man hastened to the wagon. Belle and Liberty squeezed onto the seat beside him, Belle on the outside so she could use her rifle if need be.

Bigger drops of rain were falling. Fargo tilted his head, letting the cool moisture dampen his face while he marked the position of the leading bank of clouds. Timing would be critical. Too soon, and the hard cases would cut them down before they covered twenty yards. Too late, and the rain would be so heavy Boggs wouldn't be able to see a foot in front of his face and might flip the wagon.

Retrieving his hat, Fargo dashed to the Ovaro, stepped into the stirrups, and bent over the saddle horn so the three men wouldn't catch sight of him He slid the Sharps into the scabbard, then palmed the Colt.

With each passing minute the din of clashing

thunder grew louder. Piercing lightning bolts cleaved the heavens. The drizzle steadily increased, becoming a steady downpour. And the whole time the sky became darker, ever darker.

The patent medicine man had the look of a man on the verge of unbridled panic. Phinneas held the reins so tightly his knuckles were pale and he repeatedly licked his dry lips. His dark eyes were wide, his face caked with sweat.

By contrast, the sisters were surprisingly composed, Belle wearing a determined expression, Liberty aglow with excitement. Neither showed any fear.

Fargo decided the time was right. "Now!" he bellowed, beckoning with his gun hand. Phinneas hesitated, too scared to obey, until prompted into action by Belle who jammed an elbow into his ribs.

Lashing the reins, Phinneas brought the team to a lumbering start. The bottom of the wash was just wide enough for a tight turn. A muleskinner could have made it with ease, but Phinneas was no muleskinner. He worked hard, fighting his balking animals, giving them a taste of his small whip.

It was obvious the man needed help. A jab of Fargo's heels brought the pinto close to the team. Bending sideways, Fargo gripped the bridle of the near horse and tugged, guiding it to the spot on the slope where the wagon could climb without much difficulty.

A tremendous clap of thunder caused both

horses to shy and whinny. The wagon skidded backwards a few feet. Phinneas half-rose, applying the lash of his whip with a vengeance. The team lunged forward, muscles rippling, hooves digging deep into the now-slick earth.

Fargo stayed close to them. The wagon reached the incline and he saw the wagon wheels lose traction. He worried that he had waited too long as he gave the near horse a slap on the flank that had no effect.

A jagged shaft of lightning proved to be their salvation. It struck so close his scalp tingled. It provoked the team into redoubling its efforts. Slowly, foot by foot, the wagon scaled the wash. The off wheel hit a large rock halfway up, making the whole wagon pitch like a boat in a gale. Liberty had to clutch the corner to keep from being thrown off.

Fargo pulled ahead a few yards. His head cleared the rise and all he saw were driving sheets of rain, which was as he'd hoped it would be. Behind him the wagon rattled noisily, but he was confident the noise was drowned out by the shrieking wind. He cleared the wash and paused to let the wagon catch up.

At that moment another vivid bolt briefly illuminated the scene, and in its glow Skye Fargo beheld the hard case named Jeb, not twenty feet away, holding a leveled rifle.